SEX

THE KEATYN CHRONICLES: BOOK 11

JILLIAN DODD

Jillian Dodd Inc.

ISBN: 978-1-940652-75-7

Books by Jillian Dodd

The Keatyn Chronicles
USA TODAY bestselling young adult contemporary romance set in an East
Coast boarding school.
Stalk Me
Kiss Me
Date Me
Love Me
Adore Me
Hate Me
Get Me
Fame
Power
Money
Sex
Love

Keatyn Unscripted
Aiden

That Boy Series
Small-town contemporary romance series about falling in love with the boy
next door.
That Boy
That Wedding
That Baby
That Divorce

The Love Series
Contemporary, standalone romances following the very sexy Crawford family.
Vegas Love
Broken Love
Fake Love

Spy Girl Series
Young adult romance series about a young spy who just might save the world.
The Prince
The Eagle
The Society
The Valiant

Jillian Dodd and Kenzie Harp
Young adult travel romance.
Girl off the Grid

SATURDAY, OCTOBER 18TH
ASHER VINEYARDS – SONOMA COUNTY
Ariela

THE BEAUTIFUL AND meaningful wedding I planned for Keatyn and Aiden in under three weeks was perfection. In every event I have ever done, there is always some kind of crisis—the officiant gets stuck in traffic, the cake gets cracked, the bride's dress won't zip, there's a bird in the ballroom, the best man faints at the altar, a guest has too much to drink. I even had one event that was interrupted by near hurricane-force winds. But not this wedding. It was flawless. The pinnacle of my career.

Soon I'll be helping Asher Vineyards develop the perfect on-site wedding venue as well as planning events for many of tonight's guests, but for now, I'm going to bask in the beauty of it.

As Aiden surprises Keatyn with a vintage Ferris wheel that he bought and refurbished just for their wedding, I tick off the last box on my massive *To Do* list for tonight then find Riley in the crowd just as Aiden yells out, "TRIPLETS, EVERYONE! WE'RE HAVING TRIPLETS!"

Everyone cheers. Based on the look on Keatyn's face, I'm pretty sure Aiden totally just let the cat out of the bag, and I

1

doubt she was ready for the world to know. I smile, though, happy for them.

"Triplets," Riley says to Dallas, shaking his head. "How crazy is that?"

"It's pretty crazy," I say from behind him.

He turns around, a grin on his face. As the best man, he's wearing a classic black tuxedo and looks ridiculously handsome. "The wedding has been incredible. You did an amazing job," he says. "Keatyn couldn't be happier."

"And what about you?" I dare to ask.

"Logan told me that making this wedding perfect wasn't just for Keatyn—that you wanted to show all of us that you were sorry."

"Mostly you," I say softly. "So, my duties are officially done for the night," It's well after midnight. "Would you like to dance, Riley?"

"I would," he replies, pulling me into his arms and swaying to the music.

"So tonight's supposed to be the big night," I say, my stomach suddenly filled with butterflies. After going to Eastbrooke's Homecoming last weekend, I thought we'd put the past behind us. But I gave him the note. The note I was supposed to have given him on graduation day that explained what I had to do. Why I had to go to Princeton and not come to California with him. I thought if he read it, he would understand my decision back then. But all it did was piss him off. I know I can't push things with him. I have to earn back his trust. "But I meant what I said about us not needing to decide anything yet."

"Let's go talk somewhere in private." He leads me off the dance floor, stopping to grab some champagne on the way to his room.

If he were going to tell me to get the hell out of his life, I don't think he'd bring champagne, and for the first time tonight I relax.

He pops the bottle and pours us each a glass. "Explain why you didn't send me the letter. I need to understand why you didn't fight for us."

I take a seat on the bed and take a deep breath, not wanting to relive what was the worst day of my life again, but knowing I have to for him. "I cried most of the way home. As we were pulling into our driveway, my dad finally spoke. He asked me if I told you. I said yes, and that's when I noticed I was still clutching the note in my hand. I told my dad that I had written you a letter but forgot to give it to you, so he asked what I was going to do with it. If I would send it. I checked my phone for the millionth time, but upon seeing nothing from you, I told him that I didn't know what I was going to do, but that I was surprised you hadn't called me. My dad smiled and said that the reason you hadn't is because he was right. That you didn't care about me. I decided I would keep the note on my desk for three days, and if I hadn't heard from you, I would throw it away and try to forget about you."

"But you didn't," he says softly.

"No, I couldn't do either. That's what I don't think you understand, Riley. You weren't the only one who was devastated."

"You're right. I shouldn't have given up. I should have called, and texted, and stalked your house."

"I kept praying for some kind of sign. What I should have been praying for was strength. I should have been strong enough to call you myself. I just want you to know how sorry I am. I was young, and scared, and foolish then, but I'm not anymore. I want to be with you, Riley. And I'm not afraid to say it. I still love you."

He caresses my cheek. "And I still love you."

My heart feels like it's doing flips in my chest. He still loves me. But I know the path to our happily ever after won't be easy. We aren't kids anymore. Our lives are messy. "It's not going to be easy, Riley. I still have to get a divorce. But I want you to know that I will spend the rest of my life trying to make it up to you."

"I don't want that," he says, bursting my bubble.

"I see," I say, trying to hold back the tears.

"I want us on a level playing field, Ariela. We were supposed to decide today if we want to go forward. If we want to date. What do you want?"

"You, Riley. Just you. Actually, that's not true. I want to marry you, have babies with you, and love you until you're old and gray."

"That's all I've ever wanted, too," he says, kissing me. "And I think it's about time we let ourselves be happy."

I cling to him tightly, barely believing after all this time, after all the hurt, all the pain, that I could be so lucky. "I want to be happy," I mutter out, resting my head on his shoulder.

"You know, maybe it wasn't meant to be back then. Over the last ten years, I've worked crazy long hours to make the company what it is. I gave it my life. Now we're selling it, and I can reap the rewards. I'm getting my life back. And I want to spend that life with you, kitty."

"I want that, too." His words are all I've ever wanted to hear, and they cause me to be overcome with desire. I quickly rip off our clothes, wanting nothing more than him inside me.

The world disappears, and there is only us, desperate with need, consumed by passion, filled with emotion, our bodies engaged in fervent lovemaking.

My breathing speeds up, pleasure practically coursing through my veins—*Ring.*

I ignore the sound of his phone. I'm so close—*Ring.*

Just one more exquisite thrust and I'll—*Ring.*

"Uh, I better check that," Riley says, pulling out and leaving me feeling empty.

"Who is it?" I ask as he looks at his phone.

"Shelby. I'm going to call her back." I want to say *are you fucking kidding me*, but I don't. I need to respect the fact that Riley is trying to do the right thing regarding her. But couldn't it wait?

He makes the call, and I hear her screechy voice but can't understand what she says.

"I'll be there as fast as I can," Riley says to her, grabbing his clothes off the floor and quickly getting dressed. Wait. What? He's leaving? Me. Here. Naked?

"Where are you going? What's wrong?"

"Shelby got mugged. Punched in the stomach. She's cramping."

"Is she in the hospital?" I ask.

"I don't know. I think she's at the hotel."

"Riley, it's not unusual for pregnant women to cramp from time to time. And honestly, if she's cramping and losing the baby, there isn't much you can do about it. Why don't you stay the night and go home in the morning?" Please. Please stay with me.

"The mother of my child was fucking mugged, Ariela. Sorry, but I have to go."

I make a snap decision, jumping out of bed and throwing on my clothes. In the past, I might have let him leave and sat here and cried about how fate can be so cruel, but not anymore. I'm fighting for my man. "Fine, but I'm going with you."

"You don't need to," he says. "I'll deal with it."

"Riley, I told you I would love your baby, too. I meant it."

"Really?" he says, pulling me into his arms and looking deep into my eyes.

"Absolutely," I reply confidently, because there's no fucking way I'm going to let Shelby get in the way of our happiness. Not when it's so close.

SHELBY'S BUNGALOW – SUNSET BOULEVARD

"SHELBY, THIS IS Ariela. Ariela, Shelby," I say awkwardly a few hours later when Shelby meets us at the door, but then I get to the heart of the matter. The reason I rushed here. "Are you okay? Are you still cramping? Did you call a doctor?"

Shelby throws herself into my arms and starts crying. I hold her and pat her back. "I had some spotting and cramping, but it's better now. I think I may have overreacted. I was just so upset."

"What happened?"

"I already told you, Riley. I was robbed."

"Where were you?"

"I was hungry. For McDonalds. Specifically a Big Mac. I've been having these cravings," she says, patting her stomach. I notice Ariela flinch. I'm shocked she came with me. But I love that she did. I'm hoping it means we can get through this together. That my having a baby with another woman won't affect our relationship. That she will really love the baby.

"Why didn't you call your butler and have it brought to you?"

"Because I felt like getting it myself. And I wanted some fresh air. So I went for a walk. When I was almost there, this guy jumped out from the side of a building and put a gun to my head and told me to give him my bag."

"But you didn't?"

"No! It was Fendi. Do you know how much you spent on it?" Ariela flinches again. I realize that I may not have mentioned all that has gone on with Shelby. "So he punched me in the stomach and took it."

"Did you call the cops?"

"No. I didn't have my phone with me. I left it here. I was only going to be gone for a minute."

"Then what?" Ariela asks, her voice seeming to startle Shelby. Shelby glares at Ariela and sinks deeper into my arms.

"I was shook up. Came back here. Started having cramps. Got worried. Sat on the toilet, saw blood, and freaked out."

"So you didn't tell anyone you were robbed?" Ariela says, kind of bitchily.

"I was going to let the hotel know, but then I was bleeding and that became my priority. And obviously, since you are here and not in bed with Riley, he felt it was a priority too." She starts sobbing again, pushing her face into my chest and trembling in my arms. "I've been through enough tonight, Riley. I don't need some girl you are fucking around with to harass me."

"I'm more than that," Ariela states.

"Whatever," Shelby replies with a wave of her hand. "I understand why he doesn't want us to be exclusive. I told you the last time we met, I'm okay with sharing him."

Ariela's eyes get huge. This was a really bad idea. I never told her that Shelby and I have been hooking up. A lot.

Shelby starts crying again, not at all fazed by the subject. "And the bitch of it all is that I never even got my Big Mac! Or the fries!"

I know that I should explain everything to Ariela. That Shelby was here for me when I couldn't deal with Ariela being back in my life. That she's a hell of a distraction. Yeah, probably shouldn't mention that.

Shelby looks up at me. She just looks so innocent. So young. I can't help it. I need to take care of her.

I lift her chin up and smile. "Does it still sound good?"

"Yes," she sniffles. "And a glass of wine, please. I need something to calm my nerves."

"You're not supposed to drink when you're pregnant," Ariela says. Why is she being such a bitch? Maybe because she's pissed at me now. So much for *our relationship being all that matters.*

"Looks like you've already had some," Ariela says, picking an open bottle off the table.

"Not that it's any of your business," Shelby says, "but I haven't drank any of that." She pats her stomach. "I care too much about me and Riley's little one."

"Then who did?" Ariela snaps back.

Shelby gives Ariela a curt smile. She's trying to be nice. Ariela, on the other hand, is being a real bitch, and I'm disappointed in how she's treating Shelby. I thought she was worried about my baby. I didn't expect her to come here and pick a fight. Be all judgmental.

"I had a friend over the other night," Shelby states. And I find myself feeling jealous, knowing it was probably another man.

I pour her a small amount of wine and hand it to her. "I'm going to see about getting you that burger."

"Thanks, Riley," she says, planting a grateful kiss straight on my lips.

I can't even look at Ariela as I pick up the phone and make a call.

SHELBY'S BUNGALOW - SUNSET BOULEVARD

I THOUGHT RILEY would come here. But, truth, never in a million years did I think he'd bring the preppy bitch with him. I take a few moments to size her up. She's pretty. Skinny. Has no boobs. They obviously had some sort of emotional bond. But she hurt him. Broke him. And I am going to be the woman who puts Riley Johnson back together.

She's smiling and pretending to be happy, but her jaw is set tight. So I know she's not.

Which is good. Hopefully I interrupted their night. Because I can tell just by looking at her. There's no way she fucks Riley the way I do.

And then it hits me. The next step in my plan. I need to get rid of her. Get Riley to hold me close. Then I need for us to make love. To have an emotional connection through sex. That's what he needs. It's what he doesn't get from all the girls he fucks.

I'll be honest, this is something I've never experienced. Sex, for me, has always been a means to an end—money, a place to stay, or just straight-up pleasure. Being with Bam was the closest I've ever come to experiencing something like that. Juan Fabio Martinez was passionate and a gentlemen. His accent alone would have made me wet—but I also loved the way wealth and class practically oozed out of him. It was a night I will never forget, and I will admit that I was hoping he would extend his trip so that he could see me again tonight—especially after I did an internet search on him. He's got more money than Riley, a fleet of Ferraris, and plays polo professionally.

But, alas, here I am with Riley instead. It's funny, kind of. A few days ago, I thought Riley was the ultimate prize. The big jackpot. After last night, he seems like second place. Amazing how quickly you can get accustomed to a life like this.

I think back to my shitty apartment, slide my hand down my designer clothes to remind myself just how far I've come then focus my attention to the task at hand.

Get rid of Ariela.

Make love to Riley.

He's being really sweet to me tonight. And I can tell Ariela's snotty attitude is irritating him. She probably made him bring her. I can't imagine how awkward it must be for him. I'm also feeling a little swoony. I can't believe he's on the phone getting me a cheeseburger. Now's probably not the time to mention I never eat food from there. Can't do that and keep my rocking bod.

I walk over to where Ariela is standing, pretending to need to take a seat on the couch.

"I'm going to sit. It's been an exhausting night," I say, wondering if she will reply.

"I'm sure it was," she replies dryly.

"So you're the one who broke his heart, huh?"

"Yeah, a long time ago. But I'm fixing that now."

"Not if I have anything to say about it," I say under my breath. I know she heard me, though, based on the look on her face.

RILEY SITS ON the couch between us, and I immediately snuggle up to him while the preppy bitch sits rigid with her hands in her lap.

"Riley, will you stay with me tonight, please?" I coo.

"Since you're okay, I should probably take Ariela home."

"I'm fine with you taking her home as long as you come back. Please don't make me stay alone tonight." I breathe heavy like I'm going to cry. I may even have to. "I'm so emotional."

"You were in a scary situation, not to mention the fact that you thought you were losing the baby." He touches my face gently. He really can be sweet. "Anyone would be feeling emotional."

"I've been on my own for a long time, Riley. I always take care of myself, but tonight," my voice falters. "I just don't want to be alone."

"Ariela and I can stay."

"Riley."

"What?"

"Look, I have no desire to sleep with you tonight. What I need is for you to lie in bed with me and hold me. Just hold me, Riley. It's one thing to invite her in for sex, but this isn't like that—you know what, never mind. Go home. I'll be fine alone. I always am." I turn my head away from him and start to cry silently, my body shaking.

He pulls me back into his arms while I sob. But even though I'm allowing him to hold me, I'm being stiff. Letting him know that I've backed away emotionally. Because I know that will upset him.

Do I feel guilty for manipulating him?

A little. But this Ariela chick had her chance. It's my turn.

He rubs my back, trying to comfort me. "Shh. It will be okay."

I break free of his hold. "No, it won't be, Riley. I thought I could do this, but I can't. I can't do this two women thing. I knew you were with her this weekend. And I'm fine with you having sex with her. But bringing her here was wrong. She's being a bitch to me, and if that's what our future looks like together, I don't want any part of it. I spoke to my mom today, and she's gotten her life together. I'm going to go live with her. She'll help me raise the baby."

"What do you mean?"

"I mean I don't want you in the baby's life, Riley," I reply coldly. "I'll do it myself. Without you. Without your money."

"Shelby, I don't want that."

"Well, you don't have a choice. Right now, before the baby is even born, you're choosing her over us. Go, be with her. Be happy. We won't mess up your life." I suck in a deep breath. "Seriously, go. Get the fuck out of here."

But he just sits there. And so does she.

Then the doorbell rings.

I answer the door and pick through the food, pretending to be so upset that I've lost my appetite. When Riley still doesn't say anything, I decide to force the issue. I slam the burger down on the table and march into the bedroom, slamming the door shut behind me.

I hear the bitch say, "Riley, let's just go. It's late. We're all tired. She's fine. "

"No, she's not," he says. "But you're right. *You* should get some sleep."

I hear the door to the bungalow close and instantly panic. What went wrong? Did he seriously just walk out without saying goodbye?

About ten minutes later, the door opens again. He still has his key.

Nice. I hop into bed and try to look pathetic.

He slips into the bedroom and sits on the bed with me. "I sent Ariela home. I'm really sorry, Shelby. Bringing her was a bad idea. She told me she could handle it. I didn't have time to think it all through. I just knew I needed to get here to you."

"Do you love her?"

"I don't know," he says, rubbing his face, looking stressed. "I loved her. She left me. Honestly, I haven't loved anyone since her. About a month ago, she came to town looking for me. She's married."

My eyes widen, shocked that she's acting like she owns Riley when she's married to someone else.

"I know," he says, upon seeing my surprise. "But she's filed for a divorce. She's not going back. She says she wants to be with me. That we belong together after all these years. That she loves me."

I know exactly how he feels. I've been fucked over by more guys than I can count. I reach out and take his hand. "I know how you feel, Riley. You don't trust her. Don't trust she won't throw you away again. And that's not very good for a relationship."

"She also said she could handle the fact that we're having a baby together. That she would love it. Shelby, I don't want you to move away. Please don't. I said I'd be here for you and I meant it. I proved it tonight. For God's sake, we were right in the middle of—"

He doesn't finish his sentence. He doesn't have to. "I'm sorry I ruined your night, Riley," I lie. Because holy shit. They were right in the middle of doing it and he stopped? For me? That's so fucking awesome.

"It's okay. How are you feeling? Should I call a doctor?"

"No, honestly, if I was going to have a miscarriage, there isn't much we could do to stop it. Why don't you take off your coat and lie down. I'm exhausted."

When he gets up and takes off his tie, I can't help feeling a little horny. But I can't do that with him tonight. In the morning, yes, for sure, but not tonight. I'm supposed to be traumatized.

"You look really handsome in a tuxedo, Riley," I tell him. "It reminds me of the premieres we went to. I kind of wish we could go to one again sometime. I look so different now."

"You're beautiful," he tells me, stripping down to his boxer briefs. "Do you want to change out of your clothes into something more comfortable?"

"Yeah, I probably should." I get up and strip off my clothes in front of him. Normally, I would make a show of it, and he knows it. So I have to make sure to pretend like I'm going through the motions. That I'm exhausted when I'm really feeling happy about the night's events. I can feel his eyes on me, but I don't turn around and look at him. But I do stick my naked ass out when I bend over to get a pair of baggy sweat pants and a tank out of the bottom dresser drawer. I pull on the pants, letting them ride low on my hips and turn around to face him as I'm pulling the tank over my boobs. The boobs that he loves.

He gets up and rushes toward me. For a moment, I think he's going to attack me, throw me on the dresser and fuck me. Which I am all for. But instead his hand goes to my belly. "You have a little bump. It's kind of amazing."

I immediately suck it in. "I think I'm just bloated," I say, trying to cover the fact that I am a little further along than he realizes.

"Don't suck it in. It's beautiful, really. Just think, something we made is in there," he says in awe. "I have to admit, I've sort of just been trying to do the right thing since you told me you were pregnant." His voice catches. "When you called and told me that you thought you were having a miscarriage, had you asked me a few weeks ago, I thought I would have been happy, but I wasn't. I was upset. I don't want to lose our baby, Shelby."

And that, my friends, is music to my ears. I kiss Riley gently on the lips then pull him on the bed and snuggle up with him.

Oh, Ariela. You're so going down.

And it *won't* be on Riley.

SUNDAY, OCTOBER 19TH
ASHER VINEYARDS-SONOMA COUNTY

Keatyn

"I CAN'T BELIEVE you told everyone not only that we are pregnant, but that we are having triplets. It's so early, Aiden. Multiples can cause a whole host of issues."

"You're going to be fine and our babies are going to be perfect, just like their mommy."

"Vanessa is sending out the press release today about our wedding. Do you think we should say anything? Word's going to get out."

"So, let it. When you are comfortable announcing it, we will. And not until then. You're only nine weeks. I think we should wait awhile."

"Maybe until I'm done filming. That will be right before Christmas. I'd be over four months then."

"You shouldn't even be worrying about this right now. It's your first official day as Mrs. Arrington."

"Speaking of that, Mrs. Arrington still doesn't know where she's going on her honeymoon."

"We're going to a place that means a lot to us."

"We have a lot of places we love."

"Okay, then. I thought we should start our married life by making a wish together."

"We're going to St. Croix?! Really? Ohmigawd, I get to have Inga's waffles!"

"And you get to have me."

"Mhm. That sounds good, too. But you said we are going more than one place. We don't get to stay in St. Croix the whole time?"

"Just a week. Then we're going to London, so I can show you the house I bought there. I want you to get comfortable and settled before you start working again."

"That's a good idea although, somehow, I bet you already have everything I need. Any chance Marvel will be joining us? If not, I may have to steal Inga."

He pats my stomach, actually, it's kind of a little bump. "I promise to keep you sated in every way possible. And, I thought we'd end the honeymoon with some time in Paris."

I sigh. "That sounds amazing, Aiden."

"I considered going to a resort, but—"

"This will be way better," I tell him. "I suppose we should get up and get ready for the party. Do you think there's any wedding cake left? I'm really hungry."

"You don't move. I'll be back in a jiffy with our breakfast."

"Um, is our breakfast going to include cake?"

"Marvel is making you his homemade caramel rolls this morning, along with fruit, bacon, and sautéed potatoes."

"Oh, okay," I say, trying not to sound disappointed. It's obvious that he planned this all out with Marvel in advance.

I get up to pee then brush my teeth and put on a silky robe. I look at myself in the mirror. I've had so many happy moments with Aiden, but I'm pretty sure watching his reaction when I told him we are having triplets topped them all. I can't believe he got me a Ferris wheel. He's going to be such a great dad. "You're lucky," I say to my stomach.

"Who's lucky?" Aiden asks, causing me to jump. "And I thought I told you to stay in bed."

"I needed to make sure I look presentable for my new husband," I tease.

He takes my hand and leads me back to our bedroom. There are domed trays on the table in front of the window overlooking our property and out to the ocean beyond.

He pulls out my chair as I sit down then he takes a dome off the plate in front of me, revealing a huge wedge of chocolate ganache wedding cake. "A *piece* offering," he teases before revealing the rest of our breakfast.

ASHER VINEYARDS-SONOMA COUNTY

Dawson

I WAKE UP when Vanessa snuggles her face into my chest. I'm half afraid to open my eyes. The fact that I'm with this incredible woman feels like a dream. I wasn't sure we could work through our issues.

And we both have them.

But after baring my soul to her the other night, I feel like we're closer than ever. I feel happier than I've even been. And I'm praying that moving my family into her house is the right thing to do. I know in my heart that I want to be with her, want to marry her, want everything with her, but it's a much bigger issue when you have children in the mix. The girls love Vanessa already, and I know she loves them back. Our relationship seems to have healed us both.

I brush my lips across the top of her head and open my eyes. Her long legs are tangled in the sheets, one sexy hip jutting out.

A slender arm is lying across my chest, and her hand is directly over my heart.

The one part of me I've been so afraid to give her.

She props her head up on her hand, causing the necklace I gave her to sway. I reach out and touch it.

"My favorite gift ever," she says dreamily, placing her hand over mine and giving it a squeeze.

"And I'm lying here thinking that I get to move in with you soon. Wake up with you like this every single morning."

"Wow, with all that's gone on this week, I almost forgot. Last night at the wedding, Peyton told me the crew were making a few finishing touches this morning, but that it will be ready when we get home this afternoon."

"Are you excited?"

"Honestly, I'm a little nervous. What if we hate it? What if the girls don't like their rooms? Speaking of that, when are they supposed to start school?"

"I have to call this week to find out if they got in."

Vanessa sits up and rolls her eyes. God, she's beautiful in the morning. "With the donation Captive Films made, you can rest assured the girls will be getting in."

"What do you mean?"

"I mean, private schools don't turn down big donations. That means they are in."

"That kind of makes me feel bad." I sigh. "I want the girls to get in because they are smart, and funny, and good kids."

"Are you telling me that they got into their current school without a donation?"

"Yes, no donation was required, just ridiculously high tuition."

"Or having an in?"

"Yeah, maybe. All of us Johnson boys went to the same school. Honestly, with the trouble we caused, I'm surprised they let my girls attend," I say with a laugh. My brothers and I could be a handful.

"You told me once that you'd like more children," Vanessa says tentatively, sexily biting down on her lower lip.

"I would."

"I'd really like a baby, but since I can't have children, I was considering adoption. How would you feel about that?"

"I'm all for that, too."

Tears fill her eyes. "Are you sure?"

"Yes, I'm sure. I love kids and want you to be happy."

She throws herself into my arms, hugs me tightly, and tells me she loves me. I slide my fingers across the silky skin on her hip then down to cup her ass, thinking about some morning sex.

But she jumps up.

"Oh, shit. I didn't realize it was so late! I have to send out the press release about the wedding first thing this morning, before word gets out!"

She quickly throws on a robe and leaves the room.

I close my eyes and go back to dreaming.

SHELBY'S BUNGALOW - SUNSET BOULEVARD

Riley

"I NEED TO talk to you about Ariela," Shelby says, sitting up in bed, rubbing her eyes. Nothing happened between us sexually last night, but yet it feels like it did. Waking up with her feels more intimate than ever. We went through something together, maybe. We were both scared. And I realized that I actually want this baby. "Even though you didn't tell me, I figured you were going to be with her, and that's why you didn't want me to come with."

"I went to a fundraiser just like I told you. But Keatyn and Aiden surprised everyone by getting married."

"I bet you knew that was the plan all along. Which means you lied to me." I see the hurt in her eyes.

"I couldn't tell anyone because of the press. Not even you, Shelby. I'm sorry."

"Or is it because you didn't want me there?"

"Ariela plans events. She planned the wedding. So, yes, I knew she would be there. And if you recall, we discussed that already."

"That's not really the point. You lied to me. That hurts." She rubs her stomach, causing me to feel even more guilty. "I told you, Riley, if you weren't going to be monogamous, neither was I. On Friday night, I was with someone I met here at the hotel."

"You what? You fucked some guy while you're pregnant with my child?" The thought of her with someone else simultaneously sickens me and makes me feel jealous. Am I getting attached to her in that way?

"You're not the only one with needs, Riley," she says flatly. "It's not a big deal. We were discreet."

"How did you meet him?"

"I was enjoying dessert at the bar. It was this amazing chocolate. He told me he was jealous of the pleasure the chocolate was bringing me. He was hot. The end."

"Are you going to keep seeing him? I don't know how I feel about this."

"I told you that I love you, Riley. That I want to marry you, have this baby, and be a family. You are the one who set the terms for our relationship. I'm just abiding by them." The girl has a point. *Fuck.*

"So, you're feeling okay now? No more cramping? I really think a doctor should check you out."

"I'm fine, Riley. Just having you come here means so

much." She gets tears in her eyes. "I've never had a man in my life who I could depend on."

I move closer and wrap her in a hug. "I'll always be here for you and our baby, Shelby. I promise." Her hand glides down my thigh. "But I probably need to get going."

I get out of bed quickly, because Shelby is hard to resist.

And by that, I mean with one touch, I'm hard.

I turn away from her because I don't want her to know, slip on my slacks and shirt.

"Won't you at least stay for breakfast?"

"I can't."

"So, are you going to have breakfast with her?"

"She wasn't very happy that I came here last night. She was even more unhappy that I put her in a cab, sent her home, and spent the night with you. She may not even talk to me after this."

"Well, you know how I feel about you, Riley. If you want to come back and have some fun later, call me."

I nod as I put on my shoes. "Okay. But I want you to make a doctor's appointment for this week. I think we should have an ultrasound and make sure everything's okay. And I want to be there with you."

I give her a kiss on the cheek and then get the hell out of there.

SHELBY'S BUNGALOW - SUNSET BOULEVARD

Shelby

RILEY WALKS OUT.

Which was not my plan.

At. All.

And there is no way I can take him to a doctor's appointment. The ultrasound will measure the baby to determine if my due date is accurate. And Riley is smart enough to do the math. Somehow, I'll have to go by myself.

I look up ultrasound photos on the internet, wondering what my baby looks like at this stage. When I see one where the baby looks like it's waving, I get excited. Riley will love seeing a photo like this and it's not like he's going to know the difference between a few weeks. He'll just be so thrilled to see a photo of his baby.

I think back to how he gently touched my stomach last night. The raw emotion in his voice.

Actually, an ultrasound photo might be all I need to get Riley Johnson to marry me.

THE WEDDING OF THE CENTURY?

WELL, PEOPLE.

I can't decide if I should laugh or cry about this. To be honest, I'm a little devastated.

Let's start with the official statement that I just received:

```
Keatyn Douglas and long time beau, vintner
and philanthropist Aiden Arrington, sur-
prised friends and family, who were invited
to the couple's Sonoma County home for a
fundraiser, by getting married last night.
The happy couple plans a three-week honey-
moon before Keatyn is due in London to
finish filming the last of the Trinity se-
ries movies. (Sob!)
```

I'd like to go on record and say I predicted a wedding in the very near future, but I will admit, Keatyn pulled a fast one on me.

In fact, she pulled a fast one on everyone.

When I got this press release, I literally sat here for a full three minutes with my mouth hanging open.

It's okay.

Take a minute.

It's a lot to take in all at once.

First off, I'm mourning over the loss of Keatyn and Knox as a couple.

They are soooooo perfect together. I love them!

*Not that Aiden and Keatyn don't have a beautiful (and very commercialized love story), but I still held out hope. Keatyn and Knox seemed so close when they showed up at her sisters' birthday party **together** and **without** an engagement ring.*

So, I thought—well, you know what I thought.

But, alas, I recovered quickly from the shock and, thankfully for you, did what I do best—got on the phone and unraveled all the details. I mean, there's so much to discuss!

Before I give you the skinny on the wedding, let's talk about what this really means. Knox "Sexiest Man Alive" Daniels is still deliciously single. And that's something we can all rejoice about.

So here we go.

The big question is, how was a wedding of this magnitude kept a secret?

Here's how she did it.

Asher Vineyards often holds events and fundraisers for its Moon Wish charities. Three weeks ago, local event companies were told of a "last minute event" being thrown together by Maggie Pedersen, Moon Wish's in-house event planner and Ariela Ross, a Connecticut event planner—both names Keatyn Chronicles movie goers will recognize.

Hundreds of guests received hand-delivered invitations to said "fundraiser" and were "pleasantly surprised" said one guest, to find out upon arrival that they were really attending Keatyn and Aiden's nuptials.

Because Keatyn and Knox just wrapped up studio filming and have a three-week break before reporting to their first location, the lovebirds decided it would be the perfect time to tie the knot. Friends and family were thrilled the pair, who have been together for nearly twelve years, were finally taking the plunge to matrimony. When publicist Vanessa Flanning announced the couple's recent engagement, she mentioned a springtime wedding in Paris. Since Vanessa stood up for Keatyn, we're assuming it was either a little white lie to protect her friend, or the bride changed her mind and opted for the quickie wedding.

But since our sources in Knox Daniel's camp told us to expect an announcement on Monday, we'll assume the former, because he was clearly in on it, too.

As devastated as I am, I've put my feelings behind me and have been trying my damnedest to get a picture from the event—even some grainy cell shots would suffice, but guests were asked to refrain from taking photos of the bride and groom.

I figured what the hell and called Vanessa Flanning, herself. She directed me to the wedding planner, who thankfully gave me some details.

So, here we go:

Of the six hundred invited guests, about four hundred were in attendance and the list of celebrities is too long to list. Hotels in Sonoma and nearby Napa were booked full. How none of this leaked, I have no freaking idea.

Guests were greeted upon arrival with glasses of spiked lemonade, given a wedding program, and seated on an assortment of pastel, velvet-covered vintage chairs and settees. Keatyn was glowing as she walked down an aisle scattered with four-leaf clovers and was escorted by both her stepfather, Tommy Stevens, and her paternal grandfather. The bride was stunning in a custom gown by designer Eliza Valens, which featured regal gold embroidery and a custom veil. We're told that seamstresses spent a combined total of over 1300 man hours to create the gorgeous ensemble. When I asked about the shoes, Ariela laughed and said that originally the bride was planning to wear a gold couture heel, but right before she walked down the aisle, her grandfather presented her with custom-made cowboy boots, which were embroidered in gold with symbols relating to the couple's love story.

Apparently, Aiden's nickname for Keatyn is Boots, so this is actually rather touching.

I may have shed a tear.

Or not.

I'm still in a mood over not getting an invite. I may be throwing a little temper tantrum. And I know it's early, but this calls for a stiff drink. (And later, I'll be looking for something else stiff, if you catch my drift.)

But I digress.

The couple wed just before sunset under a rustic wooden wedding arbor lovingly built by the groom. Since I can't imagine someone so glamorous as Keatyn having a rustic wedding, I was happy to hear that it was draped in the palest of silks, decorated with scads of pastel flowers, feathers, and a large vintage chandelier.

Standing up for the bride and groom were Riley Johnson, CEO and chairman of the board of the recently sold Captive Films and Vanessa Flanning, publicist of the star.

The ceremony was followed by an outdoor cocktail hour and a family-style dinner in their wood-beamed, old brick, silk draped, fairy-light lit barn. The event was catered by the couple's long-time chef, Marvel, and included a special vintage wine from Asher Vineyards. Highlights of the night included toasts from friends and family, a first dance to the song 'Sorta Like Fate' performed by the band, Twisted Dreams, and club dancing to Twisted Dreams drummer and international DJ Troy Malone's sick beats. Little sister, Emery, performed, as did numerous other friends of the couple. The evening also featured a scotch and cigar bar, cotton candy, rides on the groom's gift to his bride: a restored vintage Ferris wheel, fireworks, and in case that wasn't enough, when guests left, they found rows and rows of grapes lit by thousands of twinkle lights.

Sounds truly fabulous.

(If you noted a little sarcasm on my part, you are correct. Excuse me while I down another shot.)

Now for the gossip. With such a guest list, you can imagine the fun.

Riley Johnson was seen dancing closely with married-but-filed-for-a-divorce wedding planner, Ariela Ross.

Jennifer Edwards, who is set to star with Knox Daniels *and* Jake Worth *in* Daddy's Angel, *were seen dancing in a group, but rumor has it Jennifer and Knox have broken up. As evidenced by the fact that she ended the night in the DJ booth with Troy Malone. Troy is known to be quite the partier and what a steamy match this might be. You go, girl!*

Avery, Emery, and Ivery Stevens, the now-legal triplet daughters of Tommy and Abby, who just a few days ago were partying it up with their friends at their over-the-top birthday bash, were at the event, sans escorts. Does that mean Emery and 24-year-old bad boy rapper Treska's relationship is already over? And what about baby sister Gracelyn's recent kiss with Summer Boy crooner, Dylan?

What does it mean that they weren't invited to the wedding?

Girls? Inquiring minds want to know.

VANESSA'S ESTATE – HOLMBY HILLS

Vanessa

WHEN DAWSON AND I pull through the gates, I gasp at the sight of my home. It looks different. Sure, the terra-cotta stucco and tile roof are the same, as are the mahogany windows and iron balconies, but its harsh contrasts are gone. Added under the windows are wood and metal planter boxes filled with red begonias. The large mahogany doors are flanked by red glazed urns filled with large topiaries and set between them is a red doormat with natural colored cursive script that simply says *hello.*

I am out of the car before Dawson can come around to open my door.

"Doesn't it look so much prettier? More approachable?"

"It looks like our home now," he says, and I couldn't have summed it up better myself.

"Remember when Avery told me I needed to wear a happy dress to the Purity Party?"

"Yes," he says, taking my hand in his.

"That's how the house looks now. It looks happy."

"You look happy. That's what matters," he says, sweeping me off my feet and carrying me over the threshold.

"We're going to be happy here, aren't we?" I ask, ignoring the house and looking deep into his chocolate brown eyes. Eyes that have held the answer to that question since the day he walked back into my life.

"We are," he tells me, sealing the deal with a kiss before gently placing me on my feet. "Let's see if the inside looks as good as the outside."

"Wow," is all I can manage to mutter when I pivot in a circle, trying to take in how different it looks.

"Wow, is right," Dawson says. "It's almost hard to believe it's the same house."

The massive table in the dining room is still the same, but the walls are now the color of a Tuscan sunset. The heavy brocade fabric on the chairs and drapes has been replaced with simple cream linen. The large sideboard is overflowing with colorful Italian pottery, not priceless Ming vases, and the ornate chandelier looks more casual wrapped in metal and hanging from the wood-beamed ceiling which has been stripped of its dark stain.

I jump up and down. "It's so perfect! I can't wait to have a dinner party here!"

Dawson slips his arm around my waist and pulls me close. "And I was thinking I'd like to spread you out on that table and feast on you."

"Why don't you make a list of all the places you'd like to do me as we go through the house."

He pushes me back against the heavy wooden table. "No lists. Now."

I shake my hands in a frenzy. "But, Dawson. I. Have. To. See. The. Rest. Of. The. House. Now! Please tell me you're as excited about this as I am. This is going to be our home!"

"Oh, I'm excited, all right," he says as he thrusts his hips toward mine. He gives me a delicious kiss. "I can't help it. Your excitement turns me on."

"We've only seen the first room. Imagine how excited I will be after we see the whole house."

He nips my lip and then concedes. "You're right. That might be even better. But I will be making a list. And we will be coming back here."

"Eeee!!" I say, sounding like a teen swooning over a pop star as I lead him from room to room. Everything looks different. The dark wood has been stripped from the beams, giving them a naturally rustic look as if we've restored an old Tuscan villa and given it new life. The wall colors and draperies are softer. The ornate furnishings I thought I wanted gone have been re-upholstered and mixed with new modern pieces making the home look like it's evolved over time.

"I can't even believe this is my house," I mutter.

"I can't believe she did all this in such a short time," Dawson says. "It takes me a whole weekend just to paint one bedroom."

"She did have a whole crew working on it. I'm just—" I'm overcome with emotion. The house's makeover is similar to my own. It's the new, softer, in-love version of me. Tears flow as I turn to face the man who is responsible for allowing me to find myself again. "This is all because of you," I tell him.

"No," he says, wiping away my tears. "It's all because of you."

"But you changed me."

"No, I didn't. You were like a wilted flower. I just gave you some water."

"Now you're a gardener?"

"Well, I do like to get down and dirty with the hoes."

I laugh. "Well, it is time to go check out the master bedroom."

WHEN WE GET there, I take in the new softer version of my bedroom. It's gorgeous, almost an extension of my closet. The walls are the same pale pink. The bedding, silk in dusty pastels. The nightstands mirrored. A gorgeous chandelier above the bed. It's both glamorous and sexy. And if it weren't for the fact that I'm dying to see the rest of the house, I might slip under the sheets with Dawson and never leave.

"I think you should plant some tulips in here," Dawson says, still talking about gardening.

"Like a potted plant?" I ask.

"No, like planting two lips," he points his fingers toward his crotch, "right about here."

I swat him. "You are silly. Although that sounds fun, I really want to go upstairs and see the girls' rooms."

"Dang. I've been turned down twice now today. I'm going to get a complex." He gives me a sexy grin.

"Somehow I doubt that. Come on!"

I grab his hand and drag him up the back stairs.

At the top of these stairs is the playroom, which I knew Peyton wasn't going to change, but I peek inside anyway and immediately notice a door that wasn't there before.

"I think she made it so that Harlow's room now adjoins with the playroom." I stand in front of the door, feeling nervous. More nervous about it than any other room in the house. I want the girls to be in love with their rooms. To be happy here. "You open it," I tell Dawson. "I can't."

He wraps his arms around my waist. "Are you nervous?"

"Yes, I feel like everything, our life, is all wrapped up in this."

"If the girls hate their rooms, we'll change them."

"Okay," I say as he swings open the door.

"Ohmigawd. It's like the room of my childhood dreams. I loved horses, too." I move across the room, drawn to the cream toile paper with a pink equestrian scene covering one wall. The rest of the walls are painted a soft aqua blue, a wood-carved antique bed fit for a princess is draped with an assortment of pink, white, and teal bedding in bold patterns, and bookcases now fill an entire wall. There is a writing desk with a pink leather tufted ottoman, a round table set for tea, and a cozy reading nook with windows overlooking the stables. Her en-suite bath still features gleaming white marble, but has been made more youthful with a pink-striped wallpaper featuring gold metallic hearts.

"Harlow is going to think she's an equestrian princess, you know that, right?"

I hug myself. I'm so happy. "I sure hope so," I reply. "Do you think she will like it?"

"I think *like* is a severe understatement. She's going to go nuts. She'll be running around like a maniac."

"At least there is nothing for her to knock over anymore," I say, and that's when it hits me. "When Harlow broke that vase, that's what did it. What changed me. It's not just you. It's your girls, too. It's the life the three of you bring to this house when you're in it. It's brought the life back in me. You have no idea how much it means to me that you are allowing me to be a part of your girls' lives. I know how important they are to you. I know the three of you moving in with me is a huge step. A serious commitment. Please know that I don't take that responsibility lightly. I will do everything in my power to protect them. I know no one will ever replace their mother, but I promise to be a good role model, to love them. And you."

"For the record, life's going to get a little chaotic when they get here. You sure you're ready for it?"

"I'm positive! I can't wait. Come on, let's check out Ava's room."

I drag him across the hall and throw open the door. This room is not what I expected. It's opposite the playroom and instead of finding a soon-to-be-teen's bedroom, we're standing in the coolest slumber party space I've ever seen. There are four sets of weathered wood bunk-beds tucked into a corner of the room covered in Ikat-patterned bedding in cream, taupe, and grey. An eclectic mix of chandeliers hang from the ceiling decorated with an assortment of fringe, feathers, crystals, and shells. A massive oriental rug in silver and cream, which I recognize from the lower-level billiards room, fills the floor and is topped with sleeping bags made from faux fur. There are wicker chairs hanging from the ceiling, filled with thick cable-knit throws. One wall features a snack bar with mini fridge and shelves filled with board games. Above it is a gallery with a combination of vintage fashion artwork I've collected since I was young, interspersed with gold metallic lips and light-up letters that spell out *dream*.

"I don't even know what to say," Dawson says. "It's almost too much to take in."

"Oh, Dawson, look at this," I say, after popping open the door that now joins this room to Ava's bedroom. He saunters in, a big grin on his face when he sees that the room has been reconfigured. We're now standing in a massive closet, complete with chandelier and rows of empty clothing racks. The walls are painted the same color as my closet, a soft peachy pink that flatters your skin. There are openings on all four sides of the closet. One leading back into the bunk room, another into a cozy study zone with a built-in desk and bookshelves, and a third into a room with a TV and beanbags. The forth opens into her bedroom, which is very grown-up looking in a color palette of soft pink, glittering gold, and a muted grey.

Dawson doesn't say anything, and I worry that he thinks it's too mature. Or too much. Or just all wrong.

"Thank you," he says in a voice that is so raw and sincere, tears immediately fill my eyes. He rubs his hands down his face, wiping his eyes. "For doing this for us. Part of me is a little worried that this is too much luxury, but the other part of me feels like you're their fairy godmother. And after all they went through maybe spoiling them a little isn't such a bad thing."

"I think Peyton deserves the fairy godmother crown." I wipe my tears. "I'm sorry I keep crying. I'm just so emotional about all this."

"What do you say we hit up that wine cellar and celebrate?"

I lean up on my tiptoes and kiss him. "I think from now on, we're going to celebrate every single day."

He whispers in my ear. "Which I'm pretty sure involves getting started on my list."

MONDAY, OCTOBER 20TH
VANESSA'S ESTATE - HOLMBY HILLS
Ariela

I'M PACKING UP my belongings. I have a week off before I officially start my job at Asher Vineyards, but there's really no reason to stay in L.A. It's been well over twenty-four hours since I was put in a car and sent home by Riley, so he could *snuggle* with Shelby. He told me that he was only going to be there to comfort her. That he wouldn't have sex with her, but—and maybe it's because my husband was a liar—I didn't believe him. I could see the way she was manipulating him, playing on his emotions. I mean, part of his job is to determine whether or not someone is a good actor. How could he not see through Shelby?

Or was the drama for me? If I hadn't been there, would she have simply fell into his arms and then pulled him into her bed? She certainly looked different than the last time I saw her. Gone was the bleach blonde hair and slutty outfit, and in its place was a really beautiful woman. And the former cocktail waitress now has a Fendi bag?

Which means Riley bought it for her.

Does that mean he loves her?

I shake my head, hoping to get those thoughts out of my

brain.

Grow up, Ariela. You aren't seventeen and worried your drunk boyfriend is going to cheat on you. I'll never forget that night. Riley and his brothers were upholding the Johnson brother reputation by flirting with every female standing at Homecoming, but it was okay. Our relationship was strong. We loved being together. Being with him never got old. And I never ever worried about him being with someone else. Never felt an ounce of jealousy. Until that night. We'd been dating for a year. His brothers had been feeding him shots. A beautiful, college-aged girl was very interested in him. And he was loving it.

I stood there, tears filling my eyes, not knowing how to stop it.

So I left. Went to the lacrosse field. Sat on the bleachers and cried. We'd spent so many incredible nights in that spot, it felt like a good place to mourn what I thought would be the end of our relationship.

But Riley followed me. Begged for forgiveness. And told me that he'd never do anything to make me cry.

And he never did.

Until I came back here.

Now it seems like all I want to do is cry when I think of Riley. Either because I'm so happy I can hardly believe it, or because the situation seems fucked up beyond belief.

A line from the *Keatyn Chronicles* movie runs through my head. It was one that hit me when I was watching it. Keatyn's mom told her that she couldn't fully love anyone until she learned to love herself. I sat there in the darkened theater with Coffee Kyle holding my hand and knew that was my problem. I hadn't loved myself for a long time.

I shove the last of my clothes into a suitcase and slam it shut.

When I throw my phone in my handbag, I notice the envelope. Thick creamy paper with my name sprawled across it in

Keatyn's elegant hand. She gave it to me after dinner, and with everything that has gone on since, I have yet to open it.

I use a letter opener on the desk and find a note wrapped around a very large check.

Keatyn and I hadn't really talked about what she was going to pay me for the event, and this is above and beyond what I expected. The words written on the page draw me in.

Ariela,

> *Thank you.*
> *That's what I need to tell you.*
> *A million times thank you.*
> *For coming back into my life at just the right moment.*
> *For reviving a friendship I have missed so much.*
> *For creating an incredible wedding experience.*
> *I know this check is more than the fee you quoted me, but you earned every single penny. Every single detail of my wedding was perfection. Quite honestly, I don't know how you did it. How you were able to take an afternoon of me telling you about what I thought I wanted my wedding to be like, and three weeks later turn it into what I just experienced.*
> *I wasn't sure what to expect when I hired you, and it kind of reminds me of when we were back at Eastbrooke, when we jumped in with both feet because we didn't know better. I hope you do that with your life now, Ariela.*
> *Jump in with both feet.*
> *Keatyn*

I sit down slowly, thinking.

That's it. Today, I am going to do what I said I was going to do. Going back to Homecoming was healing for me. It helped me let some of the pain go. To remember the good times, not just the heartbreak. I know I need to do that here, too.

I'm going to all the places that were special to Riley and me when we spent the summer here. I'm going to get over it and then jump into my new life and new job with both feet.

I grab my phone and make a call.

"What's up, my beautiful boss?" Kyle asks.

"What are you doing today?"

"Maggie showed me our love nest, so I'm just here waiting for you to get back."

"Our love nest?"

"Yes, we officially have an office here at Asher Vineyards."

I can't help but smile. "Where is it?"

"A loft above the tasting room. It's cool. Lots of exposed brick and wood beams. They were using it for storage. She said we could decorate however we wanted to, but for now, I have a phone, a laptop, and a card table. Really all I need. The phone has been ringing off the hook. Mostly reporters wanting to know details about the wedding, but there are a lot of people who would like your services. Me being one of them."

"Kyle, seriously, you can't sexually harass your boss."

"I want to do more than harass you," he laughs. "But I saw you sneaking off with Riley. You still in bed with him?"

"Uh, no. It's a long story. What about you? Did you have fun at the wedding?"

"Actually, I did. I met this amazing girl."

"What amazing girl?"

"Her name is Avery. She just turned eighteen, but she doesn't act like it. She's kind of an old soul like me. Bummer that she lives in Malibu, because we talked all night. Usually I don't talk much to the girls I—"

"The girls you *what*? Tell me you didn't sleep with Keatyn's little sister?"

"I was going to say the girls I meet at parties. Usually, it's more of a hook-up situation. It was different with her. Whatever. She's cool. We might be friends. You know the only one I want to hook up with is you. How are my odds?"

"Honestly, they keep going up."

"Oh, that's not good. What happened?"

"Riley's baby mama thought she was having a miscarriage, so Riley had to go back."

"And you just let him go?"

"No, I told him I was going with him."

"Finally, the girl grows a set. Thank God."

"That's what I thought, too. But it backfired. I was pissed. It showed. The baby mama was all damsel in distress, and Riley ate it up. I'm afraid he has feelings for her."

"Don't confuse his feelings for the baby for feelings for her."

"Yeah, you're right. I shouldn't. But he also hasn't called me since he put me in a cab at her hotel so that he could spend the night with her."

"Comforting or fucking?"

"Supposedly comforting."

"I saw the way he looked at you, Ariela. The man is in love. Don't let the baby mama ruin it for you. When Tom met Gisele, his ex was a few months pregnant. It all worked out for them. It will work out for you, too. And don't be a pussy. Call him."

"Okay, maybe I will."

"So, what's next for us? What do I tell all these people who want you to do their events? Also, you should know that I took so many selfies with celebrities that my phone is blowing up. My friends are mega jealous."

"What's next for us is helping to build the ideal event space at the vineyard. And, on the side, we can take on a few events."

"Awesome. I'm going to research all these people's net worth, and I'll give you a list in order of who will probably pay us the most. I'm thinking I should get a cut."

"Just be thankful you're not making coffee anymore."

"Hey, I liked making coffee, and I was good at it."

"Did you earn what I'm paying you?"

"No, ma'am. I'll shut up now. Hey, your phone is ringing again. When are you going to be back in your office?"

I make a snap decision. "Wednesday."

AFTER I HANG up, I make another decision. I call Riley.

"Hey, kitty," he says, like he didn't spend the night with the baby mama and forget to call me.

"I hadn't heard from you since, well, since," my voice falters, but I take a deep breath and regain my strength. "And today is the day I'm going to do what I said. I'm going to all the places on the date that never ends. You had mentioned that you wanted to go with me, so I thought I would see if you were still interested in doing so," I say, sounding almost like I'm confirming a business meeting.

"I haven't called you," he says.

"I know. I figured you were tied up." Shit. Hopefully he wasn't literally tied up with Shelby. No, get those thoughts out of your mind. He told you that he still loves you. Be confident. "I understand, Riley."

"Things didn't go exactly as I expected them to when we got to Shelby's."

"With me or with her?"

"Either, I guess. Can we meet for breakfast? Talk. Then if you still want me to go with you, I will," he says cryptically. My heart sinks. If he tells me he slept with her again, I will probably die. Literally in front of him. Die.

And it'd probably serve me right.

He gives me the name of a restaurant near his office, but I say, "No. We're going to the Omelette. That's where we went back then. It's where I'm having breakfast today. You can join me there if you'd like."

"Uh, okay," he says. "See you shortly."

I put my fists together in the air like a champ. Because I

kind of feel like one right now. I have to start standing up for me.

> Triplets. And no, we're not talking about
> the newly legal ones.

Well, people.

My heart is pounding, and I'm slightly out of breath as I write this.

Just today, I got some incredible news. If you recall, I not only predicted a quickie wedding, I was the first to notice Keatyn's baby bump and her enhanced figure. (This was just seven short days ago!)

I'd like to say it was my top-notch investigative reporting, or my ability to grind on the rumor mill, but in this case, it seems the sources themselves did it. Somehow, though, it was kept quiet. You'd think wedding guests would have been tweeting and talking it about it non-stop. Because THIS IS BIG!

(As big as Keatyn soon will be!)

Keatyn is indeed knocked up, and get this—she's having tri-plets!

So picture the scene. Keatyn and Aiden have surprised their guests with a wedding. You've had a few spiked lemonades too many, and you're on the dance floor grinding against some hottie and from atop a Ferris wheel the groom cries out, "Triplets. Triplets. We're having triplets!"

Now we understand the need for the quickie wedding.

Still no word on who the baby daddy is. My money is still on Knox. But based on Aiden's excitement, rumor has it that Aiden is the baby daddy.

Speaking of Knox, I will be excusing myself early today to stalk the places he likes to frequent. I'd like to help that man drown his sorrows. (And it may involve letting him put his p in my v.)

What? I can feel your judgment through the page. You know you totally would, too, if the opportunity presented itself.

And I'm off!

THE OMELETTE – SANTA MONICA

I SPY ARIELA the second I walk into the restaurant. She's wearing a little blue dress similar to the one she wore on that day so long ago. I can still picture it fluttering around her legs as she ran through the waves. Back when things were easy. When love was enough.

Until it wasn't.

She looks up from the newspaper she's reading and smiles, causing my heart to soar. But I can't let it. I take a seat across from her. "Good morning."

"Good morning, yourself. So, we might as well get straight into it. Tell me what happened with Shelby after I left."

"Before I do that, I just have to say I was really disappointed in how you treated her."

"How I treated her? Are you kidding me? Do you not see how she is manipulating you?"

"Manipulating me? She thought she was losing our baby. She got robbed. How was she supposed to act?"

A waitress stands next to our table, ready to take our order. I order quickly for both of us just so the waitress will leave us alone.

"I don't know," Ariela says quietly, looking like she's going to cry. "I'm sorry, Riley. I just can't shake the feeling that she's using you."

"How would you feel if you were in her shoes?"

"If I were pregnant with your child? I'd be thrilled."

"No, if you met someone at a bar, went out a few times, used condoms every time, had stopped seeing each other and *then* found out you were pregnant."

She shakes her head. "I'm not sure. I guess it depends on the guy. I guess Shelby got lucky in that regard. You're a good guy."

"Would you want me not to be?"

"No." She sighs. "I have baggage, Riley. My husband cheated on me. I didn't trust him."

"I'm not him," I say simply.

"I know, but when I was there with you and Shelby, all my insecurities came back. It was hard watching you hug her."

"Imagine what it felt like for me to see you kissing your husband, looking like you'd just had sex, after you told me it was over."

She reaches across the table and takes my hand. "I'm sorry for that."

"You blamed me for jumping to the wrong conclusion, for not giving you a chance to explain, but I feel like you don't want to talk about Shelby. You never ask about her. You haven't asked when she's due. How she's feeling. What I'm feeling. You say you'll love me and the baby, but based on what happened at the hotel, I just can't imagine that working out."

"You don't think we'll work out?" she asks, looking crushed. "But at the wedding . . ."

"At the wedding my life hadn't interfered."

"What will you do if my ex tries to interfere?"

"Next time, I won't leave," I grumble.

"It's weird, isn't it?" she whispers. "That both of us feel so jealous right now. We never were that way in high school. We trusted each other completely."

"Yeah, well, that was before."

"At the wedding, you said we could start on a level playing field, but I'm not sure that's possible. Our field isn't level. And that's my fault."

"I thought we decided we are both to blame?"

"I would love to start over with you, Riley. Do you think we can do that?"

"I hope so," I admit just as our breakfast is served.

Once our food is laid out in front of us, she says, "You never told me what happened after I left."

"She snuggled into my chest and went to sleep."

"And that's it?"

I give her a hard stare and tap my foot on the ground. "Either you believe me or you don't. If you don't, there's no reason for us to even continue. I'm going to be spending time with her." She doesn't respond right away, so I dig into my food. I worked out early this morning and am starved. Ariela picks at her food, pushing it around on her plate.

"Are you having sex with her? Have you since you found out she was pregnant?"

"Yes, I have. I'm single, Ariela. I can have sex with whoever I want."

"Do you not want to be in a monogamous relationship with me?"

"I'm not opposed to it, but we've never discussed it. After we slept together that night I went to talk to you, I didn't want to sleep with anyone ever again in my life. But a lot has happened since then."

"So you want to continue to sleep with Shelby?"

"I like sex, Ariela. I always have, and I'm not going to apologize for that. I still love you. Remember when we first started hanging out, before I asked you to be my girlfriend? I wasn't talking to anyone else even though we weren't in a relationship yet. The difference now is that I *have* to talk to Shelby. I have to help take care of her. And you're going to have to be okay with that. To not get jealous and worry. The question is can you do that?"

She shrugs, finally taking a bite. I don't plan on sleeping with Shelby again, but I'm also not ready to commit to someone who is still married and who has been out of my life for the last ten years. At least not until we figure some of this shit out.

We finish our breakfast in silence. I pay the bill. We walk outside.

"So," she says, "if we're starting over, that means we don't talk about our baggage on our date. Because we don't have any. Let's pretend it's our first date. Just have fun."

"You still want to go on a date with me?" I ask, shocked.

She stands on her tiptoes and kisses my cheek. "Yeah, Riley, I do."

TUESDAY, OCTOBER 21ST
KNOX'S HOME-WEST HOLLYWOOD

Knox

I'M JUST GETTING out of the shower after my morning workout. I can't get Miss Bite Me out of my head. The texts at the wedding stopped, and I assume that's because she was with the guy she brought to the wedding. I didn't stick around to see them together.

It was amazing to me that over all these years, I'd never met her. So when I got back home yesterday, I pulled out my advance copy of *The Keatyn Chronicles* trilogy and watched every single Katie scene, fast forwarding through the rest. I wanted to know everything about her.

What I learned is that in high school she was impetuous, bubbly, and cute. She was on the dance team. She always chose the wrong guy. Tended to drink a little too much. Had the same amazing rack that still bounces when she dances.

When I got to Keatyn's eighteenth birthday party, I realized that our paths crossed on that night. She flirted with Keatyn's friend, Cush. When Keatyn suggested Cush and Aiden, who both played soccer and were both played by young, buff actors, have a face-off, Katie giggled and said, "I vote for a shirtless face-

45

off to commence immediately."

I study my reflection in the mirror. I've always kept myself in shape, but had to get particularly jacked for this last *Trilogy* movie due to the number of the shirtless scenes I have. So even though a lot of my custom suit jackets have gotten tight in the shoulders, I'm glad I look good. I close my eyes and imagine Katie's hands running down my chest . . .

My eyes fly open when I realize I've quickly become aroused—at just the *thought* of her hands on my chest.

"What the hell?" I say to my dick. He doesn't reply. Nor does he seem embarrassed.

I think again about the party, wondering what would have happened if I'd talked to her then. Would we be like RiAnne and Dallas and have been together ever since then? Would we have shared the best kiss of our life like Dawson and Vanessa did? Would she have been my green flash?

I finish shaving, dry off my face, throw a towel around my waist, run into my bedroom, and fast forward through the trilogy again, looking for a particular scene.

Okay, here it is. Keatyn and Aiden are in St. Croix.

Aiden grabs Keatyn's hand. When he squeezes it, she yells, "Oh my gosh!"

"Did you see it, too?" Aiden asks excitedly. "Was that it? I've never seen anything like that before. The sun literally turned green for a second. How did it do that?"

"Yes, I saw it! But I've never seen it do that before! It was amazing!"

"But you told me that you had seen it before."

"I think I lied," Keatyn says. Aiden cocks an eyebrow at her. "Not on purpose. I think I've wanted to see it so badly that I thought I had. But I didn't know I hadn't really seen it until I just saw the real thing."

Aiden reaches out and touches her cheek. "Kinda like the difference between loves."

"The sunset was like love?"

"Yeah, like, everyone falls in love at different times in their lives. And when you're in it, you think you know what it's like to be in love. Until you meet your true love and then you know the other love wasn't the same thing."

I fast forward to another scene. At the beginning of the first movie, Keatyn made a wish on the moon for her perfect boy, causing fans to dub the boy Keatyn would choose as Moon Boy. In St. Croix, Aiden told Keatyn he wished on the moon for his perfect girl. At the time, Keatyn was still being stalked by Vincent, so she didn't tell Aiden about her wish. Or that they made their wishes at the same time. It wasn't until the end of the last movie that Keatyn finally tells him.

"Remember how I told you about my prom night? How it didn't go according to my script, and I sat on the beach afterward?" Keatyn points down. "This is where I was sitting."

"And Brooklyn was sitting here with you?" Aiden snaps back.

She turns around, looking surprised by his question. "Well, later he came out to talk to me. That was the night when he and I sorta got started. But, I meant before that. When I was sitting here alone. It was about two in the morning. I was sad and, it sounds crazy, but I was sort of talking to the moon. Telling it what I wanted. What I didn't tell you in St. Croix, Aiden, is that I made a wish on the moon, too."

"What did you wish for?"

"My perfect boy. And I thought he was staring at the moon at that very moment, wishing for me, too. I swear, I could almost feel you."

"What are you saying?"

"I'm saying we wished on the moon at the same time. If you had told me about your wish the night we first danced, I would've let myself fall in love with you right then because I so desperately wanted it. I would've loved you even if we weren't right for each

other. When I made my wish, I didn't really understand what love was. What it should be. What it could be. I just knew I wanted it. It was like the green flash. I didn't know I hadn't felt it until I experienced the real thing."

There are tears shimmering in Keatyn's eyes.

Aiden's too. Because he swore that night he felt her too.

Keatyn smiles and takes his hand.

"Through all of it. Taunting Vincent. Taking over his company. Fighting him in the van. Trying to save him from getting shot at. Finding B. Throwing a bomb in the ocean. Getting my family back home. You motivated me. Because every time I closed my eyes and wondered if I could—if I would—survive, all I would see is you. You're my green flash, Aiden. Our moon wishes may have brought us together, but it's our hearts that led us home. To each other. I know with everything I am that you're it. My true love."

I pick up my phone and call Aiden. I know he's on his honeymoon, but I need to talk to him. I need to get my head around all of this.

"Sorry to bother you on your honeymoon," I immediately apologize when he picks up.

"It's okay. We're just hanging by the pool. What's up?"

"Maybe you should put me on speaker," I suggest. Really, I need to talk to them both.

"Okay," Aiden says and then I hear Keatyn say, "Hey, Knox! What's going on?"

"When I got home from the wedding I fast forwarded through the entire trilogy just so I could watch the Katie scenes."

"She really must have made an impression," Keatyn laughs.

"Was Keatyn playing matchmaker?" Aiden asks.

I don't get a chance to reply, because Keatyn says, "No, he saw Katie and asked me to introduce him."

"Wasn't she there with a date?" Aiden asks.

"Yeah, she was with one of those younger boys—"

"Will you two shut up!" I rudely interrupt. "Sorry, just, please, let me talk. I'm going crazy. Obviously, I'm very interested in her if I went through over six hours of footage of someone else playing her life. Anyway, today, I was thinking about how I've been in love before. How it has never worked out. And so then this morning, I remembered the green flash scene in St. Croix. And then I watched the green flash part at the end. What I need to know is if it's all true. Keatyn, did you embellish that shit to make it more romantic? Do you both really believe you made a wish on the moon at the same time? Do you think I'm crazy if I think Katie might be *my* green flash?"

"I've never had to embellish anything regarding Aiden," Keatyn says, sounding offended. "And, yes, it all happened that way. I fell for him the first day I saw him. When he held my hand for the first time, I knew. And when he kissed me at the top of the Ferris wheel—"

"You felt like you had died and gone to hottie heaven," I say, rolling my eyes.

"Knox," Aiden says, "if you feel that way about Katie, then you owe it to yourself to call her. Ask her out. It's my understanding the guy she brought to the wedding was just a date, not a relationship."

"I thought I had never met her, but I did," I admit, because this is the part that bothers me. "At Keatyn's eighteenth birthday party. If she is really my true love, wouldn't something have happened then? Shouldn't we have at least had some kind of moment or something?"

"You weren't ready for true love at that point, Knox," Keatyn says. "She would have been just a notch in your bedpost, because that's what you were into then. You had become famous quickly. Your ego was freaking ridiculous. Don't you remember what a jerk you were to me the first time we met? You weren't looking for love. Weren't even open to it."

"So you think I am now?"

"Yes. You just bought a house. You're ready to settle down. Maybe have a family. You told me all of that just the other day. *Before* you met Katie. Maybe you had to get to that point in your life before life was going to present you with the right girl."

"But what if the only reason I think she's the right girl is because I'm desperate?"

"Knox," Aiden says. "You're not desperate. You're lucky to have met someone who made you feel that way when your heart was ready for it. Don't fuck it up."

"So, I should go for it?"

"Yes, you should go for it," he says.

"Keatyn, you're being awfully quiet about all this. What do you think?"

"That's because I've been holding my hand over her mouth," Aiden says with a laugh.

"Are you sure that's really why she can't talk?" I joke. "You *are* on your honeymoon."

"Eeeekkkk!" Keatyn screams in a high-pitched dolphin sound. "I'm trying not to be too excited, but, Knox! You and Katie would be perfect for each other. She's smart. She has a wicked sense of humor. She loves excitement and adventure. She'd totally keep you on your toes."

"So it won't be crazy if I just show up there?"

"Not if you make an impression," she says.

"How am I supposed to do that?"

"You're Knox Daniels. You'll figure something out."

I HANG UP and realize a few minutes later that I don't have any fucking idea what to do. I think back to the way her mouth hung when she met me. How when women do that upon meeting me it usually goes one of two ways: they are super embarrassed and say nothing, or they go crazy overboard, screaming, touching me, and taking a million selfies.

I thought she was going to be shy, but I think her shock was more centered around a conversation she and Keatyn must have had about the question Katie always wanted to ask me. She was so adorable when she asked me about my character's lip biting. If I, myself, used that technique. How I boldly showed her that I do, indeed. And then how she frowned.

No girl has ever frowned after kissing me. I think about how her demeanor changed from shy and innocent to bold and daring as she put her hand on her hip, smirked, leaned closer to me, and said, *What I really wondered is if you do it when you kiss somewhere lower.* Then I was the one standing there with my mouth open. I quickly recovered though, asking if she'd like to find out. But she had a date. And although I wanted her to ditch him and be with me, looking back, it says something about her character that she didn't. The girl has some morals. And I respect that.

I also can't stop thinking how she described the men—well, the younger guys—she dates. How they were *good for fun and intensity, but not big on finesse.* I want nothing more than to prove to her that I am the best of both worlds. I want to show her I have all the finesse my age and experience dictates, but that Knox Daniels has plenty of intensity. I also can't stop thinking about the long, hot kiss we shared when I pushed her up against the side of the barn. How I begged her to come to my room. How even though I've never done what she asked me about, it's all that is on my mind now.

I reread the cute texts she sent me.

I love how bold she was. How she told me *if* I was good in bed, I could take her to D.C. this weekend. Hell, I'm going to do a lot more than that.

But how?

A text pops up on my phone screen.

Keatyn: *Aiden will kill me if he sees me texting during our honeymoon, but if you haven't figured something out, watch*

The Bachelor. *She's obsessed with that show.*

I have heard about the reality TV show, but I have never seen an episode. I might know someone who has, though.

I get dressed quickly, run downstairs, and yell into my assistant's office. "Talk to me about *The Bachelor.* What do you know about it?"

"Oh gosh!" Missy exclaims, her eyes wide with excitement. "Which season? I mean, there have been so many good ones."

"I'm wondering more about the structure of the whole thing. What happens on the show? What about the show do you like?"

"Well, it starts with a bunch of girls who want to win the bachelor."

"*Win* the bachelor? So, it's not about love?"

"Sometimes its about love. I mean, it's supposed to be about finding love, but most people love it because of the drama that goes on to get to that point. Have you ever had two girls fight over you?"

"Yeah, I guess."

"Imagine twenty women fighting over you, and you are all living in the same mansion. And to get to know them, you go on dates with them. And if you like them, you give them a rose so they can stay. Girls who don't get a rose have to leave the show."

This piques my interest. "What kind of dates?"

Most of them are group dates where they get to spend time, hopefully, with the guy. They can be anything. Olympic style events, an activity, a cocktail or pool party, at some point they go home to meet certain girls' families, but my favorite part is when they get an invitation to the fantasy suite."

"I like the sound of that. What do they do there?"

"Well, first they travel there in high style. A private plane, I think. Then there is an amazingly luxurious and romantic suite and when they go in there, the cameras are off so they can get to know each other better." She lets out a wicked laugh. "*If* you know what I mean."

"So that's when they sleep together?"

"The official word is that they *talk* all night. I suppose some do. But for others I'm sure it gets physical."

"So the fantasy suite is a big deal?"

"Yes."

"So roses, dates, the fantasy suite, what else?"

"The final rose ceremony is when he gives the girl he loves a rose and then proposes."

"That's what I want to do then. Shower her with roses. Take her on a date. Meet her family. Take her to a fantasy suite. Then a final rose ceremony with a proposal. Will you help me set it up? And make sure the press doesn't find out?"

"Wait! You want to do *all* of those things?"

"Yes, I do."

"Oh, Knox. She's not worth it. She was cheating on you. You can't be serious about—"

"I'm not proposing to my ex-girlfriend. I met someone new." I can't help but smile widely just thinking about her.

"Look at you," she says, swatting my shoulder. "You're all smiles. Who is this girl? Where did you meet her? How long have you been dating?"

"Her name is Katie. She's a school teacher. We were at the wedding together."

"As in Keatyn and Aiden's wedding? I heard it was beautiful."

"And a big surprise. In large part because of what you leaked to the press the morning of the wedding."

"I wish I could have gone."

"You would have loved it. It was perfect. How is your grandma doing?" I ask. Her grandma fell and broke her wrist, which is why she couldn't come to the wedding.

"She's good. Tough old bird, that one," she says. "So, Katie was your date for the wedding? Why haven't you told me about her?"

I take a deep breath. She's going to think I'm nuts. But she can't say much. She and her partner were married only three months after they met.

"No, she was actually there with someone else. I met her for the first time at the wedding."

"Wait. Let me get this straight. You want to propose to someone you met three days ago, when she was on a date with someone else? Are you crazy?"

I nod and grin like an idiot. "Actually, yes. I am. I'm crazy about her."

She frowns and studies my face. She's been my assistant for over ten years and probably knows more about my life than I do. But after a few moments, her face softens and then she grins. "I don't think I've ever seen you like this, Knox. You're smitten."

"I am. Completely. I can't wait for you to meet her. She's funny, and cute, and sweet, and a little ornery."

"Did you sleep with her?"

"No," I say. She listens carefully as I animatedly tell her what all went down. Her connection to Keatyn. How we briefly met years ago. The question she asked me.

"So she told you she'd go away with you this weekend? Have you spoken to her since then? Do you have a plan? Is she meeting you there? You picking her up?"

"I haven't spoken to her since. I want to surprise her. Maybe at her school. Like I want to show up, give her a shit ton of roses, whisk her away."

"You've been friends with Keatyn for far too long. That sounds like something out of a freaking fairytale."

"That's exactly how I want it to be."

"You go pack. I need a few minutes to think this through logistically."

WHEN I COME back down thirty minutes later, she says, "Did you pack a tuxedo?"

"Of course."

"Perfect," she says, grabbing the carry-on bag she always keeps packed and shooing me out the door. "We've got to get to the airport."

The whole way to the executive airport, she's making phone calls and crossing things off a list. By the time we're buckled up, she says, "I can't believe we're doing this."

I don't bother to reply. I know it's right.

VANESSA'S MANSION – HOLMBY HILLS
Ariela

A SLIVER OF light peeking through my curtains wakes me up mid-morning. I turn my face toward Riley and open my eyes. I told him last night when he brought me home that I shouldn't let him spend the night. It was supposed to be our first date, after all—the first date of grown-up Riley and Ariela. Although breakfast was tense and awkward, the rest of the day went better. We rented rollerblades and skated down the boardwalk. We walked hand-in-hand at the Santa Monica pier, stopping in shops, eating junk food, playing games, and going on all the amusement park rides. We flirted and kissed. But I told him I wouldn't sleep with him on the first date. He argued that if it is truly the date that never ends, he had to stay. So we made out and fell asleep in each other's arms.

I rub my hand across his firm bicep and am immediately aroused. If I don't get out of this bed, the rest of the date will involve a whole lot of sex. And as much as I want that to happen, I want to spend time with him in other ways more.

I try not to wake him as I slide out of bed, but he grabs my waist and pulls me back toward him. "Morning, kitty," he murmurs into my hair.

"Morning," I say, melting into him. That's one thing that hasn't changed a bit. Riley causes physical reactions in my body that no one else can, particularly as I can feel the pressure of his morning wood against my leg.

"We going to continue the date that never ends by spending all day in bed?" He has a smirk on his face, and his hair is messed up, which makes him really hard to resist.

"You know how I feel about that, Riley. Besides, we still have a lot to do."

"I'm tired. We did a lot yesterday, and I ate way too much sugar."

"I know, but I learned so much about you."

"Like what?"

"Well, you have a personal trainer named Raul, who is your assistant Tyler's partner. Your favorite color is still green, but you hate green ties, favoring purples and blues instead. You've developed a love for sushi, even though you wouldn't touch the raw stuff in high school. You order Thai at least once a week. You've switched from cheap beer to craft. You have an obsession with designer shoes and watches. And you and Dallas still get high."

"And I learned a few things about you, too," he says, as his hand slides across my waist. "I learned your knees are still ticklish. That the color of your eyes has deepened. That you don't blush as often when I make dirty comments. Your favorite color is still pink, but you haven't worn it since we broke up.

Your hair smells like lemons and cream instead of strawberries, and you can handle more than one glass of wine without getting tipsy."

"That's why I don't want to spend all day in bed with you, Riley. We already know that's still the same. And today is going to be unseasonably warm, so it's the perfect day to spend at the beach."

"You want to try to surf?"

"I never really got the hang of it, but I liked going out on the board and watching you. We can take a picnic. Watch the sun set. Have a bonfire."

"Then I can chase you under the pier," he says. "And you know what will happen when I catch you."

CAPTIVE FILMS - SANTA MONICA

Vanessa

I'M IN KEATYN'S office putting dates into a spreadsheet for the *Daddy's Angel* marketing campaign when I realize something. I haven't had my period for a while.

I check back over my calendar and realize I'm at least a week late. And since I can't get pregnant, my missing period must mean something is wrong.

But, what?

I do a quick internet search and discover lots of reasons why I could be late. Except . . . I don't have excessive weight loss or gain, nor do I suffer from an eating disorder.

I'm not ill.

I don't have emotional stress. At all. I'm happier than I've ever been in my life right now.

JILLIAN DODD

I'm not on the pill. No need.

I don't use illegal drugs.

My heart drops.

That leaves ovarian cancer.

I suck in a big breath, trying to calm myself down. We're supposed to find out today if the girls got into their school. We'll find out when they start and when they will be moving into my newly redecorated home.

Where we're supposed to be a family. The family I long for. I'm finally happy. Loved. Could life be so cruel to me?

I can't have cancer.

But I know it's the only logical reason. It's been two years since I've had my yearly exam. And I know that's really bad, but after what happened, I just couldn't face my doctor again. I couldn't go back to the place where it all ended for me.

And now, I'm going to pay for it.

I'll die.

The girls will once again be motherless, and I'll never get to hold a baby in my arms.

Dawson flings the door open, startling me. "I just got the call! Their first day of school will be November the third. Less than two weeks! I'm so excited to tell them." He studies me. "What's wrong?"

"I have something in my eye," I say brusquely, feeling crushed. I prayed every day that the girls would love the school and want to move here. I even promised them both they could adopt a pony. Now I'm scared.

"Oh, okay," he says. "Anyway, just thought you'd want to know."

"Um, actually, Dawson, I'm right in the middle of this. Can we talk later?"

"Uh, sure. Want to have dinner tonight and celebrate?"

"I have plans tonight, sorry," I lie, causing him to leave my office looking disappointed.

But I can't do it to his girls. I can't become a mother-figure to them if I have cancer. I can't and I won't put them through something like that when they've been through so much all ready.

And that includes Dawson.

WEDNESDAY, OCTOBER 22ND
PRIVATE SCHOOL - CINCINNATI
Katie

"THOSE OF YOU who are done with the test need to be reading quietly until the bell rings," I announce to my class. The kids are all hyped up because when they get out of school today they get a five-day break. I glance at the clock. Only twenty more minutes. Then I'm supposed to go to dinner with Kevin before we have to be back for parent-teacher conferences tonight. Not that many of the parents will be here. They just don't seem to come once their children go to middle school and have multiple teachers.

I'm not sure what to do about Kevin. He's cute and damn good in bed—actually better than most of the guys I've dated that are his age—but after my encounter with Foxy Knoxy, I just haven't been as attracted to him. I can't even bring myself to kiss him.

Damn Knox Daniels and his stupid hot kiss. What the hell has he done to me?

I glance at my phone for the millionth time, hoping to find a text from him. Was he drunk? Was he not serious about seeing me this weekend? It's Wednesday. I told him I'm off on Friday.

That means if it's going to happen, there should be some planning going on. Right?

Maybe I should act like a grownup and just text him. Yes, that's what I'll do.

> **Me:** *Hey, um, were you serious about maybe getting together this weekend?*

Ten minutes later.

No reply.

Okay. That's my answer then. It was just a stupid kiss.

Except, it wasn't.

It was the hottest, most passionate kiss of my life. It was a soul-searing, earth-shattering, ridiculously incredible moment. It was more than just a kiss. It felt like . . . something I've never experienced before. Like I was finally home. That all the boys I have kissed in the past had only kissed me so I would understand Knox's perfection and what it meant.

I open my top desk drawer and look at the tabloids I bought at the airport on the way home from the wedding. One that Knox and Keatyn happen to be on the cover of. God, he's so fucking beautiful. And those damn dimples.

"Miss Katie," the school secretary says, peeking her head into my classroom. "Principal Martin would like a quick word with you in her office."

My class goes, "Oohh," like I'm in trouble.

"Can't it wait? Class will be over in a few minutes."

She shakes her head furiously. "No! It absolutely can not wait. No. It can't wait. You must go now."

"I can't just leave my class."

"Oh," she says. "I will take care of them. You go." She shoos me out the door.

I look back at her, thinking she's acting very strange as I make my way to the office. I'm not even to the door when Principle Martin pulls me inside.

"There you are!" She grabs my hand, drags me into her office, and practically man-handles me into a chair. Then her eyes get big, and she rushes over to her window and shuts the blinds.

"What's so important that you pulled me out of class right before the bell?" I ask.

She wrings her hands together, acting nervous. Oh, shit. Does she know about me and Kevin hooking up?

"Look, before you say anything, I'm going to end it with him." Her eyes get huge, like I just told her I was having an alien baby. "Kevin is sweet and all but—"

She lets out a big rush of air as she drops to her chair. "I didn't bring you here to talk about Kevin. We, um, we have a bit of a situation. Uh, with the parent-teacher conferences. There is a parent coming in who, uh—" She stops speaking as the bell rings, ending the school day. "Anyway, as I was saying, there is a parent coming in who wants to talk to you about their child."

"That's what parent-teacher conferences are for," I say in a smart-ass tone. "You know, so parents and teachers can talk."

She glances at her phone, looks annoyed at it, and continues. "Yes, yes, well, of course, but this is a more sensitive subject, so I'm thinking maybe when the, uh, parent comes in that possibly we should have the school counselor involved."

"Which student is it about?"

"Oh, well, I'm not exactly sure," she stutters out. "The parent didn't give me their identity. Just told me of the situation."

"What situation?"

"Well, the one with the child, of course," she says.

"And what situation is that?"

Her phone buzzes and she looks down. "Oh, time to go," she says, getting up.

"But, we didn't finish."

"No time, now. You need to get out of here, go get some dinner, so, uh, you can be back here in time for the conference."

"With the unknown parent who has something sensitive to discuss with me?"

"Exactly," she says, brightening and linking her elbow in mine. "Come. I'll walk you out."

Principal Mary Martin is actually a good friend of mine. We do a girls' night out at least once a week. She is acting very strangely. But I know she's having trouble with her ex-husband, and conferences always stress her out. Maybe that's all it is. Or maybe there's something more going on with this parent she was talking about.

"Why don't you come to dinner with me? You seem like you could use a drink," I suggest as we make our way down the hall to the main entrance, which is unusually empty. Guess the kids couldn't wait to get out of here.

"Me? Oh, no. I'm perfectly fine, besides," she says, slinging me out the front door. "You're going to be busy. Look!"

And look I do.

What I see is like something out of a movie. The front lawn is filled with students who cheer as the doors open. Each one of them is holding a single red rose. Even some of the parents are out there. All of them with roses.

"What's going on?" I ask as a sudden horror fills me. This looks like a proposal. A school-type proposal. Is Kevin going to propose? Is that what has Mary so excited? She must be in on it. No, it must be something else. Surely, Kevin is not going to propose. We've only been hooking up for about a month. He's never mentioned the word wedding, not even when we went to Keatyn's.

"What the hell is this?" I whisper out of the side of my mouth.

She throws her hand in the air dramatically and everyone yells out, "Will you accept this rose?"

Then the crowd parts, and at the end of the sidewalk stands Knox fucking Daniels. In a tuxedo.

I stand frozen wondering if I fell asleep during class and am dreaming. If I am, I sure as hell don't want to wake up.

Knox smiles, flashing those dimples, and walks toward me. He has one hand behind his back and actually looks a little shy.

"You owe me a big explanation," Mary says, elbowing me, "as to why you didn't tell me you met and—God can only hope, what else you did—with Knox Daniels."

I try to swallow, but my throat is too dry. My heart is beating frantically in my chest. But I'm smiling back at him. He's here. I think it's possible that he's really freaking here. But I still don't move.

He takes the steps two at a time, and before I know it, he's standing directly in front of me. "So, will you accept this rose," he asks, pulling a single long-stemmed red rose from behind his back.

I try to say yes, but no words come out, so I just nod.

"Kiss!" the crowd yells.

That I can fucking do, I think, as I throw my arms around his neck and crash into him.

His tongue flits across my lips, and as I start to open my mouth, I remember where I am. Who is watching.

As I pull away, he says, "Sorry, I came too soon. I couldn't wait until the weekend."

I whisper naughtily in his ear. "When we get back to my place, that better not happen."

"What better not happen?"

"Coming too soon."

"Aw, sugar. What am I going to do with you?" he chuckles.

"I can think of a few things," I tell him, my eyes wide with unabashed desire.

"Be careful, teacher," he says. "Lots of little eyes and ears here."

All I can think about is getting him back to my place as soon as possible. But then I remember that I have conferences. "Um, it's great that you're here and all and this is amazing, but I have to work tonight."

"Actually, you don't," Mary says, handing me my bag. "We're all covering for you. Now, you two go have some fun! I don't want to see you back here for a while."

"It's conferences. You said no one could miss them. Not even if we were sick."

"Well, that's before Knox Daniels showed up, dear. You take all the time off you need. I'll teach your class myself if I have to."

"Thank you," I reply gratefully, giving her a hug.

She whispers. "He literally bought every rose in the city. For you."

Knox takes my hand and leads me toward a waiting stretch limo. On the way there, the students all start giving me their roses, and by the time we get in the car, a large bouquet fills my arms.

PRIVATE SCHOOL – CINCINNATI
Knox

THE SECOND WE get inside the limo and the door is shut behind us, our lips collide, the roses tossed aside. Her tongue slides into my mouth, taunting me with wickedness yet to come. She makes quick work of my tie, pulling it off me.

And as much as I want all this to happen, I need more. I must fucking be in love with this girl.

"Slow down there, sugar lips," I say, ending our kiss and

65

leaning back.

"*Sugar lips* not just *sugar?*" she pouts, making me wonder if I said something wrong.

I rub the pad of my thumb across her lush lower lip, wanting nothing but another taste. "I called you sugar lips because your lips taste like a delectable mix of honey and candy."

This causes her to grin. She pats the bouquet of roses lying strewn across the seat. "So what's with all the *Bachelor* references? And who told you, Maggie or Keatyn?"

"Keatyn."

"You talked to her on her honeymoon?"

I raise an eyebrow in her direction. "Well, some things can't wait."

"You know, I don't get you. You were all flirty at the wedding. Seemed disappointed I went back to my date. Told me we were going away this weekend then nothing. No texts. No calls. Nothing. I assumed we weren't . . ."

I take her hand in mine and gently caress it. "I had a few things I needed to wrap my head around first."

"That's such a guy answer," she laughs. "What does that even mean?"

"It means that our kiss by the barn—"

"We were up against the barn," she challenges.

"Yes, we were. That kiss was—"

"Earth shattering," she says, finishing my sentence. "It was the kind of kiss that destroys you. I'm actually mad at you about that kiss."

"Why's that?"

"Because I haven't been able to kiss another man since." My heart nearly stops beating, I'm so happy. I was so worried she went back and, well, you know, with that other guy. It's been driving me insane thinking about her with another man. I don't think I've ever felt such jealously in my life.

And it makes me smile.

She sees my grin and says, "Oh, you like that do you?"

I plant a sweet kiss on her lips. "Actually, it makes me very happy. I was incredibly jealous when you left me to go back to him. So, what did you think of my entrance?"

"I had no idea it was you. Like that thought didn't even cross my mind. I was freaking the fuck out because I thought he was proposing. He's watched *The Bachelor* with me before. Knows I love it."

I wince. "You were that serious?"

"No, we weren't, but I just couldn't figure out what else it could be. It felt like a proposal—a big crazy gesture. I was pretty happy when I saw it was you. But I never would have guessed it."

"What would you have done if I had proposed?" I dare to ask.

"I would have fucking said yes," she says with a giggle. "Hell, I may have to marry you, or risk never having a sex life again."

"Do you remember meeting me at Keatyn's eighteenth birthday party?" I ask her. I don't know why this has been bugging me, but it has.

"Briefly, yeah, we were introduced, like, when you walked in."

"How come we didn't have a moment then like we had at the wedding?"

"You thought we had a moment?"

"You *know* we had a moment."

"Hmm. It was probably because I was dating someone, sort of. He was my high school boyfriend and was going to college, and we were stuck in that spot of not knowing if we'd stay together. We ended up not."

"Was that Bryce?"

"How did you know that?"

"I may have watched all your parts in the movies when I got

67

home."

"Oh, God, so embarrassing." She covers her face as she blushes.

I remove her hand and kiss her cheek. Then her neck. "Not embarrassing. You were too cute."

"Cute and dumb. I want to say it was because I was young, but honestly, I still do dumb things."

The car stops. "Looks like we are here," I say.

She narrows her eyes at me. "How do you even know where I live . . . never mind. Keatyn?"

"Maggie," I tell her, helping her out of the limo and up the stairs to her apartment.

When she opens the door, she stands in shock. Every flat surface, nook, and crevice is filled with bouquets of roses.

"You really did buy out all the florists in town, didn't you?"

"Well, I'm trying to make an impression, in case you can't tell."

"And what kind of impression is that, Mr. Daniels?" she asks, pulling me inside and taking a big whiff of the beautiful scent. "Gosh, it smells incredible in here."

"I'm glad you like it." I'm pretty sure I'm beaming.

"So . . ." she says, grabbing my lapel and pulling me close. Her soft lips brush against mine. "Are there flowers in the bedroom, too?"

"Let's go see."

"Eek! They are so pretty. And there are rose petals all over the bed. Wait. How the hell did you get into my apartment?"

"Well, my assistant, Missy, called and explained the situation. I don't think they believed us until I walked into the leasing office. I thought one of the girls was going to faint."

"And they just let you in? Because you're a celebrity? Did they at least make you show some ID?"

"Yes, they did. And they accompanied Missy, myself, and the two floral delivery trucks. Then they locked up after us."

"Well, I guess that's okay then." She seductively slides onto the bed, beckoning me to join her. Why am I not throwing myself on top of her and fucking her brains out?

Because I like her. Fuck. I'm nervous.

And although sleeping with her here surrounded by rose petals was my original idea, Missy texted me a few minutes ago and told me that the word was out. That photos were being posted on the internet. She said she hopes that it will stay contained to the local vicinity, but she can't guarantee it. And that we would be best to head out tonight, not in the morning. I definitely don't want Katie to have to deal with the paparazzi yet. And I'm not ready for that either. I need time alone with her. Just the two of us.

So rather than pounce on her delicious body, I find myself pulling her back up. "We're going to date...*Bachelor* style."

"You mean I have to compete for your love?"

"Actually, no. This is Knox-style. You've already won this round—thus the roses. We're skipping the drama and going straight to the good stuff."

"The sex, hopefully?"

"No, the dates. I want to take you on a fun date. I want to meet your family. And I want you to experience the fantasy suite."

"That all sounds fun, Knox, except the part about my parents. My mother passed away. Dad got remarried. I never see him anymore. His choice. No other family to speak of. What about you?"

"My father passed away a few years ago. My mother is currently on a mission trip. I help raise money, she goes and does good with it. I can't wait for you to meet her."

"When will she be back?"

"Not until the holidays."

"So what are we going to do?"

"Well, we can't stay here, I know that."

"Why not?"

"Because word is out about the floral stunt I just pulled, and I don't want to be hounded by the paparazzi. We're going to stay one step ahead of them."

"How are we going to do that?"

"Well, sugar, that part is easy. We just need your passport. I looked around and couldn't find it."

"You searched my apartment?" she asks, looking horrified.

"You have quite an impressive collection of vibrators," I smirk. "Something to help when the finesse is lacking?"

"Exactly," she says. She moves into the kitchen, opens the freezer, and takes out a Ziploc bag. "My passport."

I laugh. "That is the one place I didn't think to look."

"Well, the idea is it won't burn if there's a fire. Don't know if that's true or not. So what should I pack?"

"Nothing," I tell her.

"So I'm either wearing the work dress I have on or nothing?"

I pull her into my arms and kiss her. "I have taken care of everything. Let's go."

VANESSA'S ESTATE – HOLMBY HILLS

Dawson

I SHOW UP at Vanessa's house after work. I haven't seen her or really heard much from her for a couple of days. She said she was busy with clients, but things feel off between us. Like there's something she's not telling me. Or that I did something to upset her. Although, I can't imagine what it would be. This past weekend was incredible, and her house turned out so well—

exactly what she wanted.

We have a nice dinner in the newly decorated kitchen, but the conversation feels forced, and I hate it. So I just ask.

"You seem distant. What's going on? Everything okay with work?"

"Yeah, work is fine," she states, not responding to the rest. I notice that she really hasn't eaten any of her food.

"Are you having second thoughts about me and the girls moving in? If you are, it's okay, Vanessa. I know things between us have happened fast. If it's not the right—"

"You might be right about that," she says, setting her fork down.

"Um, which part?"

"All of it. I'm not sure if the girls moving here is a good idea."

"Then why did you have their rooms done?"

"I just can't do this right now, okay?" she yells at me and then storms off. "Please, just go home!"

What the hell is going on? Did I misread the situation? She had the house redone for us. She's been excited. Now that it's a reality, she's changed her mind?

Maybe that's it. It was fun thinking about it and planning it, but now she doesn't know if she can do it. Or she just doesn't want to.

I consider trying to talk to her, but decide maybe it's best if I don't right now.

I might say something I would regret. Because I'm fucking pissed. I told the girls we would be moving in. I told them they would be so surprised to see their rooms.

Now, she's made a liar out of me.

I march to the front door, fling it open, walk out, and swing it shut with all my might, causing the house to shake.

I DRIVE TO my house and then go for a walk on the beach,

trying to both clear my thoughts and calm myself down. But it doesn't work because I can't figure out what went wrong. Is she just nervous? Does this mean that we're over? Or is it just too much too soon?

I don't have any answers.

So I go back to the house and try to get some sleep.

At little later, I see that she texted me and wants to talk.

Well, fuck that.

KATIE'S APARTMENT - CINCINNATI

Katie

I CAN'T EVEN believe this is happening. Knox Daniels— smoking hot, sexy, incredible Knox Daniels—is in my apartment. After our hot kisses in the limo and the romantic scene he created, I figure we won't leave here for days.

I even spread myself across the bed, a clear invitation to take me, but instead he pulls me up, makes me get my passport, and leads me out of my apartment.

He doesn't even let me pack a thing. No sexy lingerie, no toothbrush, no makeup. This is going to be a disaster. Thank goodness, I have a little touch-up makeup kit in my purse at all times.

It's weird, the more we talk, the more I joke around with him, the less I think of him as my Foxy Knoxy dream guy, and the more it feels like he's just Knox. He's sweet and adorable. His kisses are ecstasy. And the best part is knowing that our kiss at the wedding affected him as much as it did me. It's crazy to think I could be dating a movie star, but when we kiss, what he does slips away and all that is left is us.

After leaving my apartment, we are whisked to an airport where a private jet is waiting for us.

"Where are we going?" I ask.

"You'll see," he says then kisses me.

And doesn't stop kissing me for the entire flight—even though I have made advances that suggest I'd like to do much more.

WE LAND IN the District of Columbia just as the sun is setting over the Washington Monument. It's a little cloudy, and the sky is bathed in shades of pink and blue.

A limousine meets us on the tarmac, and in a short time we're pulling into the Four Season's private entrance and are taken up an elevator by a bellman.

"Give us the tour," Knox says, although he probably stays here every time he's in town. "I've never stayed in something so extravagant."

And that makes me like him even more. He holds his elbow out for me, and I link my arm with his. Tightly. I can't even believe I'm here.

A butler opens a set of double doors and says, "Welcome to the Royal Suite."

The foyer itself is a breathtaking room, polished wood on the walls, glittering mosaic on the floor. "Look at the twinkling lights on the ceiling," I screech, pointing upward.

"Those are Swarovski crystals twinkling above you. If you'll follow me," the butler says, leading us into a beautiful dining room that will seat at least ten. It's decorated in soft colors and is flooded with natural light. He taps on one of the windows and says, "Bullet resistant glass."

"Hope we don't need that," I whisper to Knox, but the butler overhears me.

"It also is wonderful for insulating you from the noise of the city. From the dining room, we have a large open salon. It features a sitting area, a library, a formal living area, and a media room."

"How big is this place?" I ask, stunned.

"Around four thousand square feet." I beam at Knox, who beams back as we follow the butler into a stunning bath. "The bath features a large soaking tub, mother-of-pearl tile, double vanity and large shower. Beyond that we have the master bedroom."

"I could live in just this room," I blurt out. "Actually, who am I joking, I sort of do. This room alone is the size of my whole apartment!"

The butler finishes the tour by showing us the private workout room as well as a sprawling private terrace featuring its own fire pit. The doorbell rings. "That will be your bags. Would you like us to unpack for you?"

"No, thank you," Knox tells him, handing him a folded up bill. "That will be all for now."

As soon as he leaves, Knox picks me up and twirls me around. "So what do you think?"

I reply with a kiss.

"What do you want to do first?" he asks, setting me down on my tiptoes.

"Well, technically, you cheated." I smirk and raise my eyebrows at him. "You weren't supposed to be allowed to bring me to D.C. until you had proven your worthiness."

"Oh, now I get it. You only want me for my body," he says, pulling off his shirt and revealing a perfectly sculpted chest, thick abs, and an impressive V-line, but what really catches my attention are his arms. I reach out and glide my hand across a muscular bicep.

"I just might. Gosh, you've been working out."

"I always work out, sugar."

"Yeah, but I saw your last movie. You weren't this big. At least you didn't look this big on screen."

"Everything is bigger up close. Why don't I show you?" he says, sweeping me off my feet and lying me across the chaise in the bedroom. Then he stands up and slowly strips for me.

First his belt, which he snaps at me when he undoes it. Might have to have some fun with that later.

He's going way too freaking slow. I've been imagining this night for years and have become obsessed with thoughts of it since he kissed me. I can't wait any longer. I unzip his pants, push them the fuck down, and pull him on the bed with me, not even bothering to take off anything other than my thong.

THREE HOURS LATER, I am completely naked, trying to catch my breath. "Oh wow," I say, plopping back on the bed. That was—"

"Hopefully more finesse than you're used to," he drawls.

"It was more *everything*. I just—wow. I have no words. And I teach English. I always have words."

He takes my hand in his, holding it slightly above us and staring at the way our hands look together, like it's the most interesting thing in the world. "If you could do anything, sugar lips, what would you do?"

"Like I could quit my job, move to Costa Rica, stare at the ocean, and write books kind of thing?"

He rolls to face me as he traces my collarbone with his finger. "So that's what you'd do? Write?"

"Yeah. I have a bunch of ideas. Stories I've started, but never finished. I always get busy. Or think it's a dumb idea."

"What kind of books?"

"Children's. Middle grade or young adult. I had a dream about a place you got to through a secret door, sort of like Narnia, but the world was very different. The kids go back and forth between the worlds. That kind of thing."

"That sounds really cool. You should totally do it. Want to hear a secret?" He smiles, flashing his dimples. "I wrote a script.

75

It's something I really never considered doing before, but I was so inspired by this particular storyline that it just rolled out of me. And it's totally different from the blockbuster action films I've been doing. It's this romantic time traveling story about love that transcends time."

"It sounds amazing. Maybe you'll let me read it sometime," I tell him, still barely believing that I am lying in a bed with Knox Daniels conversing about life in a ridiculous suite having just spent the last three hours—gosh, do I even dare think it— making love. The first time was fast, furious, needy—animalistic and primal. The second time was a little less rushed, but equally intense. Then he slowed down and proved his powers of finesse by taking me to places sexually that I can honestly say I've never been before. And he did do the lip biting thing down lower, but he didn't bite me, just sort of gave it a little tug after getting me all worked up. It was more like a kiss on the nose. Quick, sweet, but the fact that he told me he'd never considered doing it there, that he'd never experienced it with another woman, only heightened my arousal. Like it wasn't already sky high.

"I just bought a house in Sonoma County. Not far from the vineyard," he says, drawing my attention back to what he's saying. Although it's sort of hard to pay attention because his hand is now gliding up between my thighs. Part of me wonders if I can take any more. The other part of me can't wait to find out.

"Really? I mean, don't get me wrong, it's gorgeous there, but it doesn't seem like there would be much nightlife for a bachelor like you."

"Keatyn and I both put our lives on hold to do the *Trinity* series. I'm ready for a slower pace." The hand stops gliding, and his finger taps my skin. "A place to call home. Do you like the area?"

"It's beautiful. I enjoy visiting, but I think I might get bored." I shift my body slightly, hoping he will keep moving his hand upward.

Instead he sits up, puts his elbow out, and leans his head against his fist. I'm in a lust and ecstasy induced haze. Is it wrong that I can barely focus on his words when his hand is so close? "But Keatyn is there. Your friend, Maggie. Wouldn't that be fun?"

"It would be more fun because you would be there, probably," I coo, deciding to take matters into my own hands—and by matters, I mean his dick.

"Could you write somewhere like that?" he continues.

"If I robbed a bank, sure."

"What if you shared my bank?"

I let go of his dick and sit up straight. "What do you mean?"

He gives me a lazy smile. The kind that makes me slow down and enjoy just talking to him. "I wondered if you'd ever considered moving, like there, with me."

"Are you asking?" I say, trying to keep my eyes from popping clean out of their sockets.

"Depends on your answer," he drawls sexily, moving his hand from my thigh up to caress my face. I want to tell him he's getting colder, but I refrain out of shock that we're discussing living together.

"You don't think it's too soon to talk about that?" I ask. Are we really talking about this?

"If I were younger, maybe, but I'm not. I know what I want, sugar. And it's you."

"I don't know what you mean," I stutter out.

"Do you want kids? Because I really do."

Have Knox Daniel's baby? Um, yeah. "I love kids. I guess I just thought if I wasn't married by now, it probably wouldn't happen for me."

"You're not even thirty yet."

"I know there's still time. It's just the baby daddy prospects have been weak. And I don't want to have a baby without being married."

"Old fashioned girl, I like that." He leans forward and kisses my forehead, causing me to melt.

"Why did you ask me if I'd move in with you?"

"Because, sugar lips, I'm pretty sure I'm madly, passionately, deeply in love with you."

"Then the answer to your question is yes. I'd love to move in with you."

THURSDAY, OCTOBER 23RD
CAPTIVE FILMS–SANTA MONICA

Riley

I CAN'T FOCUS. Shelby keeps texting me, wanting to see me. Ariela sent me a picture of her and Kyle working on her new office. Which pissed me off. Kyle is young and buff and good-looking. And Maggie says he totally is crushing on Ariela. Maybe I should let him have her. I honestly just don't know what to do about Ariela. We had fun on our nearly forty-eight hour date.

Until the pier.

It killed me that she wouldn't make love to me under it. The night before she told me that she couldn't sleep with me because it was our first date. Which was cute and I played along, doing nothing but kissing her until we both fell asleep. But it was the pier. I mean, what was the point of reliving all those memories if you aren't going to recreate the best part? And her reasoning was bullshit. That if we're starting over, we shouldn't have sex until we're ready? That we waited back then. Which made no fucking sense since we've done it numerous times since she's been back in my life. But when I called her on it, she said, *Look, Riley, I can't sleep with you if you're sleeping with Shelby, too. You know that Collin cheated on me, and I am just not an open relationship kind of girl. I'm willing to wait for you to figure things out, but I'm not willing to do that with you until you do.*

Which really pissed me off, because she put it all on me. And she has no right to do that. She's still married. Just sleeping with a married woman goes against everything I believe. And she's said absolutely nothing about her divorce. I don't even know if or when it will happen! Maybe the spark that Ariela used to have isn't the same. Maybe being in an unhappy and unfulfilling marriage for so long has sucked some of the life out of her. I know it's still there, buried deep down. Probably the same place where my heart has been buried. She was right. She is definitely not the same girl I fell in love with. And I can't decide if that's a good or bad thing.

I guess it's just different. And that's part of why it's so hard. Half the time it's like no time has passed between us. The other half is filled with turmoil and rife. Part of me doesn't even want to try with her. Between the pier and the way she treated Shelby, I just don't know how in the world we could ever work.

Or maybe I'm just telling that to myself because I'm afraid she'll break my heart. Again. Just her rejection under the pier cut me deep.

I stand up quickly, knowing I need to do something, but not sure what.

CAPTIVE FILMS–SANTA MONICA

Dawson

"ARE YOU OKAY?" I ask my brother when he barges into my office and sits down in the chair in front of my desk.

"I don't know. Everything is so fucking complicated. My head is a mess." He runs his hand through his hair, looking frustrated. "I just don't understand why whoever is in charge of running the universe decided to bring Ariela back into my life and have Shelby get pregnant all at the same time."

"How much longer until you can find out if you're the father?"

"Fuck, I don't know. A couple weeks, I think. They said we could find out as early as eight weeks. I think she's six weeks right now. The bitch of it all is I didn't want the baby. Like not at all. And I maybe secretly hoped it wasn't true. Or that she'd lose it. But then she called me crying the night of the wedding and was afraid she was having a miscarriage"—he stops and puts his hand to his chest—"it's weird, but I was upset. I didn't want her to lose my baby." He rolls his eyes at himself. "I make no fucking sense."

"Well, the pregnancy was a surprise, Riley. You didn't plan for it to happen. Trust me, I know. That takes some getting used to."

"You loved Whitney, though."

"And what about Shelby?" I ask, studying him closely.

"That's what's worrying me more than having the baby, to be honest. I have feelings for her." He stands up and starts pacing. "Why in the fuck do I have feelings for her? It was just sex."

"You think you love her?"

He shakes his head. "I don't know. She's confident and bold all the time, but she was so vulnerable and upset the other night. It got to me, emotionally. And it upset her that I let Ariela come with me, which made me feel even worse."

"Ariela went *with* you to see Shelby when she thought she was having a miscarriage? Are you an idiot? You had to know that would never work."

"Yeah, well, I didn't. Ariela told me she loved me and would love the baby. That she was going with me. I thought it might be helpful having another woman around."

"But then the claws came out?"

"Yeah, Ariela's. And *that* I did not expect. She was downright rude to Shelby. And it pissed me off. Of course, it probably didn't help that we were literally mid-fuck when I stopped because Shelby had called three times in a row."

"Oh boy. So it was an emotionally charged situation. How did you handle it?" He stops pacing and sits back down.

"I sent Ariela home. Shelby wanted me to spend the night with her because she was so upset."

"Understandable," I agree. "But I'm sure that didn't make Ariela too happy."

"No. It didn't."

"When you spent the night with Shelby, did anything happen?" I ask, gently.

"We talked. I held her. She fell asleep in my arms."

"And what about when you woke up?"

"I wasn't going to have sex with her!" he fumes. "She had been cramping and stuff. Even bleeding a little."

"Just asking, bro." I hold up my hands. "Don't jump all over me."

"See. That's what Shelby does to me. I freaking care about her. And it's fucked up."

"It's not fucked up that you would grow to care for the mother of your baby, Riley."

"I get why you married Whitney now. I didn't before. But I do now. I'm sorry for all the shit I gave you about it," he says, slumping down. "Why is this happening to me?"

"Are you thinking about marrying Shelby?" I ask, trying not to show my shock. "What about Ariela?"

"I don't know," he says quietly. "I just don't know."

"You don't have to decide until you know," I say, hoping it helps him feel less stressed. "If you're feeling this way, date them both. Figure out which direction you want to go. You know that you and Shelby are sexually compatible, but you need to see if you like her as a person. If you get along in that respect. If you love her. With Ariela, you feel the love, but it's an old love. You need to get to know the Ariela she is today. The only way you can do that is to date them both."

"I'm not sure Ariela will go for that."

"Ariela doesn't have a fucking choice but to go for it," I tell him. Now I'm all worked up. "She came back into your life with no warning whatsoever. After ten years! She broke your heart. Broke all our hearts, really, when she broke yours. She has been in California for one month. She can't expect you to just drop your life because she decided she had a shitty marriage. That's not fair to you. And she's still married. We weren't raised that way," I say, reminding him of our religious upbringing.

"I know. I feel that Catholic guilt every time I sleep with her. So what should I do?"

"You're Riley Johnson. You do whatever you want. *Whoever* you want. Ariela has you all fucked up. Until something happens that makes *you* want to change things, then you should be true to yourself. And if you are, you'll make the right decision."

"Thanks, bro. I needed that," he says, looking me in the eye and reminding me of when we were young and I was just his big brother. The brother who always looked out for him. He gets up and gives me a hug. "You're right. That's exactly what I need to do."

He leaves my office looking less stressed than when he came in. Which makes me feel good. Well, sort of good. I'm upset about Vanessa. I haven't told the girls that we're not moving in with her. Haven't been able to tell them there will be no pony adoptions.

But then I see the envelope I was given when they an-nounced the sale of Captive Films. The one that is supposed to tell me how much my stock options were worth. I'll be honest. I really didn't pay attention to it being a benefit, because I never imagined they would sell. Keatyn had asked if I'd like to be CEO of the new company. If I'd like to use the funds to buy into the new Captive. I sort of figured that's what I'd do with the money. But now I don't know.

I hate to call her on her honeymoon, but I pick up the phone anyway. Then I realize I don't need to talk to her, I need to talk to Dallas. He's the one who handles the financial side of Captive.

I walk out into the hall. "Hey, Tyler, is Dallas in today?"

Tyler looks at his iPad. "Yes, he'll be here for a few more minutes, then he's got a round of golf scheduled."

"Perfect," I say then head to his office. I find Dallas sitting behind his desk dressed in a very conservative suit and tie. Not his usual golf attire. "Hey, you got a minute?"

"Sure," he says, pointing to the couch. "Take a load off while I finish up this email."

A few moments later, he sits in the chair next to the couch, puts his feet up on the coffee table, and says, "So, what's shaking?"

"I wanted to ask you about the new Captive Films. Keatyn asked if I wanted to run it. I was wondering about some of the logistics. Like will I continue to office here?"

"No, as part of the deal, Front Door Films is assuming our lease. It was something I managed to slide in the contract that allows us to get out of this large space without having to buy out the lease, and it had the bonus of allowing all the employees who move with the company to keep their offices. If you take the job as CEO, you and I will decide together where we want the offices to be. It takes me nine minutes to get from my house to the country club. I'd like to have the offices somewhere in between. You're going to have to move closer anyway or your girls will have an hour and a half commute to and from school.

And as it is, it takes me an hour to get from my house to our offices here in Santa Monica."

"It would be nice to be close. It'd be a lot easier to attend school events, maybe even pick up the girls from school some days."

"You're going to need a nanny. I'll have RiAnne call you with the service we use."

"That'd be great," I say, but all I can see are dollar signs adding up. My salary here is good, but I'm going to need to find somewhere else to live. "Look, I'll just lay it on the line. You know about my financial situation and the sweet deal Keatyn gave me to come here. With the girls moving here . . ."

"It's understandable that you'd want to know the package details before you accept an offer."

"Yeah, exactly. It wasn't really an issue when I thought that the girls and I were going to move in with Vanessa, but now . . ."

"Trouble in paradise?"

"Yeah, I guess she changed her mind or something. I don't blame her, though. It's a big commitment taking on two kids. I'm just glad she decided now before we all moved in, but now I'm not sure what to do."

He holds his hand up. "Say no more. I negotiated a month-to-month lease on the Malibu property. I thought if the girls came out, you would want to choose a home yourself. Would you like me to call our realtor and set up some places for you to look at?"

"So, Captive will continue to lease me a house?"

Dallas smiles. "Unless you want to buy one yourself. If you don't want to invest your shares in the new Captive, you certainly could afford to do so."

I squint my eyes at him. "What do you mean?"

"Did you open the envelope?"

"No. I haven't been here very long. I figured I'd let myself be surprised with what it is, whenever it comes."

Dallas lets out a laugh and slaps his knee. "Dawson. You're a Johnson. It's time you got over the fact that your wife left you broke and realize you're back on top."

"I am?"

He gets up, goes to his laptop, and makes a few clicks. A printer starts up, spitting out a document. He waits for it to finish then hands it to me.

"Keatyn and I hammered out the details of your compensation as CEO of the new Captive before she left for her honeymoon. I don't have your contract prepared yet, but these are the highlights. You're looking at a healthy salary, large bonuses, a piece of the company whether you buy in at the beginning or not, 401K, long-term health and life plans, country club membership, car allowance, and an optional home lease."

I stare at the numbers on the page—more than triple what I'm earning now. Which means, I can definitely afford to stay here. "That's a big bump," I say, numbly.

"Keatyn and Riley want to go back to doing what they love, and I'm ready to play more golf, which means we are trusting you to run the company. You cool with that?"

"Yeah," I smile. "I am."

"Good." He glances at his watch then grabs his briefcase. "Speaking of that, I've got to get to the club. I've got a cold beer waiting for me and some brand new PXG clubs that need to be broken in."

As we walk by my office on his way out, he says, "Open the envelope, Dawson. Then let me know if you'd like to invest the money in the new company so you'll have a bigger piece of the pie, or if you want to buy a house or something."

"Uh, okay," I say, my curiosity now piqued. Surely it's not enough to buy a house. But before I go into my office, I stop at Tyler's desk again.

He looks up at me. "Yes?"

"Can you come in my office for a second?"

"Why, Mr. Johnson, I thought you'd never ask," he says, picking up his iPad and sauntering in ahead of me.

I take a seat at my desk. "I'm assuming Keatyn spoke to you about coming to work for the new company?"

"She did, but she really didn't give me many details. Like at all. She's been holding this all very close to the vest. What do you know? Give me the skinny."

"The check that you got, for your shares in Captive, was it much money?"

"One million seven hundred and fifty-two thousand dollars."

I'm a little blown away by that number, but Tyler has been Riley's assistant since he started working here. "Are you considering retirement?"

"Are you kidding? I'm spending it! Well, not all of it, but I might be considering a new place to live. I mean real estate in this town is usually a good investment. But I don't want to do that until I know where the offices will be. I heard Front Door is taking this place over."

"They are. And I was asked to be CEO for the new firm. I don't think I'd be nearly as successful if you weren't a part of the new company, too. But it would mean you'd be working with me."

"I'm already working with you, Dawson. Who do you think gets everything done around here?"

I can't help but laugh. "I probably should rephrase that. Will you work with me at the new Captive?"

Tyler puts his hand on his hip. "I have demands."

"Like what?"

"I get to create my own title."

"You don't want to be called an executive assistant anymore?"

"No, I was thinking something like *Supreme Keeper of the Realm*."

"I can live with that." I nod, trying to suppress my smile.

"And I'd like to help pick out our new offices. I assume Peyton Moran will do the decor, but I'd like a say, for functionality purposes."

"Deal."

Both my phone and Tyler's iPad beep with a text. He's quicker to react. "Oh, lookie here at what Mr. McMahon just sent us. A link to an office space in Beverly Hills. On Wilshire." He holds up a street view of the building for me to see. "Be still my heart! It's across the street from Saks!"

"Where do you live now, Tyler?"

"Raul and I have an apartment here in Santa Monica. But we'll definitely need to move now. What about you? You can't commute all the way from Malibu. Do you want to go house hunting together?"

"You picked out my place in Malibu, didn't you?"

"Of course."

"Then, yeah, Tyler. I would love your help. At least to narrow things down."

"Dallas said the deal will close in thirty days. We'll have our checks a week after that." While he's talking, he's on his iPad. "Holy Batman! Will you look at this!"

"What?"

He turns his iPad toward me. "Mr. Johnson, we have an important business meeting to attend. Right now. Come on!"

"Where are we going?"

"We're moving on up!" he sings, dragging me out of the office.

He's on the phone, but he points at my Ferrari in the garage and says, "You're driving." Then he gives me directions while he converses with both Raul and a realtor. Apparently something just came on the market that *screams Tyler*.

It takes us over an hour to get there because traffic is a bitch. No way could I do this every day with the girls. They would be miserable. *I'd* be miserable.

We meet a realtor outside the building of Tyler's interest.

"It's a ten minute walk to all the Rodeo Drive shops and restaurants," the realtor tells us after we make our introductions.

"Can you even imagine?" Tyler gasps. "I may need a clothing allowance, too, now that I think about it."

"How about just a nice raise?"

"Have I told you that you are my favorite Johnson brother?" He grins, but adds, "Don't tell Riley that."

The realtor takes us into a beautiful condo and mentions that it's being sold furnished. From that point on, it's Tyler running around in a designer-decorated-induced frenzy.

"Look at these black and white marble floors! They are so classic! And the crown moldings! Oh, my stars, magenta tufted club chairs! Purple fur pillows! Arched French doors! This chandelier! Glass-fronted Sub Zero! A workout room. A terrace! Raul will die, I tell you. D.I.E. Die!"

And then finally he says, "I'll take it."

The realtor looks a little shocked, but recovers quickly. Tyler makes an offer that is just slightly below asking price and then he turns to me and says, "Done."

And I know in that instant exactly why he is so good at his job. He's not afraid to make a decision when he knows it's the right thing.

I wish I was that confident in my personal life.

CAPTIVE FILMS—SANTA MONICA
Riley

WHEN I GET back from my brother's office, I call Shelby. "Would you like to have dinner tonight?"

"Uh, sure. What time?"

I glance at my watch. It's only four, but I'm having a hard time concentrating. "I'm done for the day. Half hour work?"

"I'll make sure to be ready," she says seductively.

"Ready for what?"

"Just ready, Riley," she says cryptically, which I hate to say turns me on. Shelby usually has really fun surprises.

When I get there, she opens the door wearing a pale peach silk robe. The robe is tied and covers her completely from the waist down, but the top is open, revealing a see-through lace nightie underneath. Her nipples are hidden, but I can see their outlines under the sheer robe. She looks beautiful. I swallow hard. Shelby is the ultimate temptation, and I am free to do whatever I want with her. That thought alone causes my dick to harden.

"I thought you'd be ready for dinner?" I need to get her dressed and to a restaurant before I do something stupid. Something stupid that will undoubtedly feel so very good. I really do need to get to know her better and just stop falling into bed—or wherever—with her.

"I wasn't sure if you wanted to eat out," she says, sitting down and crossing her legs, causing the robe to fall open and reveal a clean shaven pussy at literally the same time she said *eat out*. Now it's all I can think about. "Or if you wanted to stay here."

"How are you feeling?"

"I told you every day on the phone this week that I'm feeling great, Riley," she smiles. "Thanks for asking. How was the big date with Ariela?"

"How did you know about that?" I ask, sitting a relatively safe distance away from her. Okay, maybe not safe enough. When she leans over to converse with me, I get a full shot of her incredible cleavage, which just keeps getting fuller as her pregnancy progresses.

"Tyler told me when I called your office."

"Oh," I say, suddenly feeling uncomfortable. The good news is it calms my dick down. "It was nice."

"Nice?" she asks, arching one eyebrow. "I'd expect with you it would have been naughty. Or is Ariela not as naughty as I am?"

I gulp and try not to think of all the dirty things I've done with Shelby, because the answer is no. Ariela is not as naughty.

"Let's go out for dinner," I quickly suggest, because shoving my cock into Shelby certainly isn't going to help me decide who I love.

Thankfully, Shelby stands, presumably to go get dressed.

Except, she doesn't go. She undoes her robe, letting it fall to the ground and revealing a sexy lace nightie that leaves nothing to the imagination. *Fuck.*

"Maybe we should stay in," she coos, trailing her finger under my chin. I don't move. I don't dare. Because I know what my next move will be. At least when I have sex with Shelby I don't have to feel guilty. With Ariela I feel like I'm committing a sin or something because she's still married. When did my life get so fucking complicated? Easy. When Ariela walked back into it. And part of me still hates her for that. Even though at Homecoming I told her we should let the past go, I just can't seem to get fully past it.

When I don't say anything, Shelby slips onto my lap, straddling me. "You seem tense."

"It's just—"

"Ariela?" she asks, as her lips graze across my neck. "What you two do when you are alone is none of my business, just like it's none of her business what happens when we are alone. Plus, she's still married."

When her lips touch mine, all rational thought ceases. All I feel is desire. I try to compare the animalistic hunger Shelby brings out in me versus how Ariela makes me feel like I could never be with anyone else again. *True love's fuck*, Dallas called it. Except here I am. With someone else. Wanting her and needing her. I think it's just that my feelings for Ariela are so complicated. With Shelby they are simple. I just want to fuck her.

After she pulls my cock out of my pants and lowers herself onto it, she stops moving and holds my gaze, running her fingers tenderly through my hair. She kisses my temples, my jawline, my lips, then looks into my eyes again.

I smile and really look at her. She's beautiful and sincere. And Lord help me she has a sweet pussy. She's not moving, but she's internally tightening it against my dick. It's driving me crazy.

"I want to show you something," she says. "It's probably a little unconventional to be attached like this when I do, but it seems fitting of our relationship." She leans over and grabs an envelope off the end table. "Take a look."

"What is it?"

"I went to the doctor on Tuesday. I was able to get an appointment, and I know you wanted to come with, but Tyler told me you were with Ariela, and I wanted to be respectful of your relationship even if she isn't respectful of ours."

"What did the doctor say? Is everything alright?"

"Everything is perfect," she says, giving my dick another soft squeeze. "Open it and you'll see."

I do as I'm told, pulling out a dark photo. An ultrasound photo.

"That's our little bundle of joy. Can you believe how teeny it is but how it's so perfect?"

"It looks like it's waving," I say in awe, studying every single detail.

"You should have seen it. It was kicking and flailing its little arms. And I heard the heartbeat. The doctor says it's perfect.

That I'm doing well. That the cramping and little bit of spotting was probably just stress-induced."

I hold the photo up to the light as tears fill my eyes. "This is our baby," I mutter. "It's amazing."

Shelby kisses me and looks deep into my eyes. "I love you, Riley."

"I love you, too," I say back, and it's quite possible that in this moment I mean it.

"Oh, Riley! You don't know how much that turns me on!"

Then she proceeds to show me just how much it does.

CAPTIVE FILMS-SANTA MONICA

Dawson

TYLER DROPS ME off at the office and then leaves early to tell Raul the good news. I go back to my desk and decide to look through some real estate listings. But then I see just how much homes cost in the area. My increased salary could cover the mortgage payments no problem, but I don't have enough for the hefty down payment that would be required for the loan.

I glance at the envelope and decide to open it.

When I do, I'm overcome with emotion. It's almost the exact amount that Whitney lost. And I know it's not a coincidence. I pick up the phone and call Keatyn.

"Hey, Dawson," she says.

"I just opened the stock options check. You can't do this."

"Yeah, I can."

"It's too much, Keatyn."

"Dawson, when I hired you, I didn't know that we'd get the offer on the company. It was just a random amount we chose as a safety net for you. You had a similar buy-out clause in the change of control agreement at your last job. My grandpa always says if you give good, you get good back. Maybe the deal with

94

Front Door was kinda like that. The whole thing is amazing for Aiden and me, too. We agreed on 1.6 billion. I owned fifty-one percent of the company. We're pretty much set for life now. And, because of it, my grandparents decided to take what they had planned on leaving to me and started some kind of foundation trust thing that for the next twenty years all the earnings from it will go to the Moon Wish foundation. And then it will pass tax-free to our children. It's pretty amazing all the good that will come from it. So feel good about it, Dawson. You deserve every penny."

"I can buy a house now. For the girls."

"But, I thought—"

"She changed her mind."

"Vanessa changed her mind about you and the girls moving in? When? She sent me photos of their rooms. She was thrilled with the way they turned out. She was super excited."

"I don't know. I didn't stick around long enough to hear her excuses."

"Dawson, if you love Vanessa, you have to stick around long enough to hear her excuses. It's called being in a relationship. It doesn't make sense. Something is going on with her. Please, talk to her and find out what the real reason behind it is. And if you don't move in with her, we'll have Tyler find you a place closer to the girls' school. I'd rather you invest the money in the new company. I promise you it will be a good investment." She pauses. "I take that back. You, more than anyone, know that you should never go all in on any one investment. Give us half. Invest the rest. Let us do a long-term lease on a house. I wouldn't buy until you are sure the girls and you are going to love it."

I let out the breath I hadn't realized I'd been holding. "You really think she didn't mean it?"

"I really think she didn't mean it, Dawson. Talk to her."

"Thanks. How's the honeymoon? Where are you anyway?"

95

"St. Croix. It's incredibly relaxing, but we'll be in London on Saturday, in case you need anything. Talk to you soon."

I set my phone down, cover my face with my hands, and say a grateful prayer. I'm lost in thought when I hear my door open.

I look up, startled, and see Vanessa. Usually when she comes to work here she's wearing a sexy suit, designer heels, and red lipstick. But today, she has on very little makeup and is wearing yoga pants and a baggy sweatshirt. Clothes I've never seen on her. She also looks like she's been crying.

I quickly take her into my arms. "What's wrong, baby?"

She immediately starts crying. Hard. Her body is racked with emotion. Pain.

"What's wrong, Vanessa? Tell me what happened."

"I think I have cancer," she stutters out. "That's why I can't let you and the girls move in. I don't want them to get attached to me if I'm going to die. It wouldn't be fair to them. They have already been through so much."

"Oh, honey," I say, my heart both dropping and soaring all at the same time. I hold her tightly and let her cry it out.

When she stops sobbing, I walk her over to the couch and make her sit down. "Why do you think you have cancer? Have you been to the doctor? Had tests?"

"No. I researched my symptoms online."

"And what symptoms are those?"

"My period is a week late. I have fatigue. I can't remember what else, but I have all the symptoms. I went through every single reason why my period could be late, and it's the only one that fits." She starts crying harder again. "And . . . I . . . Just . . . I know I was supposed to go get my yearly exams. I know that early detection is key. But . . . After . . . Everything . . . That happened. When I found out I couldn't have children. I just . . . I just . . . Couldn't. Make myself . . Go back there. It's been two years."

"Have you made a doctor's appointment?"

"No." She throws her arms around me and sobs into my chest. "I'm so scared, Dawson."

"Let's call his office now and get them to squeeze us in."

"Us?" she sniffles. "You'll go with me?"

"Of course, I will. I love you. Whatever this is, you're not going through it alone."

She sobs again. "Bam wouldn't even go to my obstetrician visits with me when I was pregnant."

"Well, we have already determined that Bam is an idiot."

She starts laughing through her tears while I sigh with relief. Cancer, if that's what it is, I can handle. Her not loving me, I can't.

THE CRAB-ST. CROIX

Keatyn

AIDEN PICKS ME up off the chaise and carries me into the ocean. "What are you doing?"

"Getting you wet," he teases.

"I think you've been doing plenty of that." I grab his face and kiss him. "You've barely let me out of bed!"

"Well, Boots, it is our honeymoon. What do you expect?"

"It's been an amazing week, Aiden. I'm getting excited to go to London, though. I miss Bliss."

"I miss her, too. But she loves Marvel and they both will be joining us in London."

"Are you sure you won't show me even one picture of the house you bought? I'm dying to see it. I still can't believe you bought it without me. We always do everything together."

"We'll see it together for the first time."

"What? You bought it sight unseen? Are you crazy? What if it's in a bad neighborhood or by a train station or something?"

"You will love the location. It's in Chelsea, which is the area you love best. We've been looking for the right property to purchase there for quite a while."

"Look, dolphins," I say, getting distracted. Aiden kisses me.

"Dolphins love you. I think you may be descended from mermaids."

"That just totally made my life," I tease. "I wanted to be a mermaid when I was growing up."

"Well, the mermaid in you will enjoy one part of your new London home."

"Which part?"

"The spa."

"Like there's a spa in the building? Is it a flat?"

"Nope. Single family. The spa is on the lowest level. Trust me, you'll love it."

"If we're going to spend all our time at the vineyard, why a house in London? I mean, we could have just leased something while I was filming there."

"Um, well, I was offered an incredible opportunity to team up with a top London chef to open a restaurant, wine tasting room, and retail space. The location is incredible."

"Let me guess, it's in Chelsea, too?"

"Yeah. I was going to tell you everything when we got there. Show you both the house and the location. We've agreed in principal, but haven't signed the contracts. Wanted to do it in person. But I've been rethinking things a little since the wedding. I mean, triplets."

I wrap my arms around his neck and give him a kiss. "It's a wonderful surprise, Aiden. For a lot of years, you've worked around my dreams. It's time we start following some of yours. Is the house suitable for children? Is it big enough?"

"Uh, yeah."

"Aiden! How big is it?"

"About eight thousand square feet."

"Holy shit! That's way bigger than the house at the vineyard."

"I know. It's also an architectural masterpiece. I really couldn't pass it up. The location is perfect. The photos are perfect. I also may have sent someone over to check it out."

"Your sister?"

"Well, originally, I sent her over to see the restaurant location. The place is gutted—a blank space. I wanted her opinion on it. She's way better at visualizing that kind of stuff than I am. While she was there, I got the call about the house. So she toured it. Told me if I didn't buy it, she was going to."

"She and Damian already have a place over there."

"Yeah, well, it doesn't look like this."

"Can we leave tonight?"

He kisses me again. "So you want to skip the barbecue brisket, cheesy potatoes, and cornbread Inga is making us for dinner?"

I scrunch up my nose. "Maybe not." I look into his gorgeous green eyes. "Aiden, are you scared about having three babies?"

"A little. Are you?"

"Yes. What if we can't handle them? What if they turn out to be brats? What if they aren't healthy? What if I have complications and die? Then they will be motherless, and you'll marry someone else, and what if she's nice to them when you are around but mean to them when you're not and they grow up all messed up and end up on drugs and—"

"Stop right there." He pulls my hand to his lips. "Everything's going to be fine, Boots. I promise."

"You can't promise that."

"Fine. Then I promise whatever challenges we face, we'll face them together, with all the love we have."

I get tears in my eyes. "I love you, Aiden. You have no idea how incredibly happy you make me."

"Oh," he says, sliding his hand between my legs. "I think I do."

FRIDAY, OCTOBER 24TH
THE ROYAL SUITE-GEORGETOWN

Knox

I'LL BE HONEST. Katie and I didn't leave the hotel suite yesterday. We were either naked or wore the hotel's robes, dined on room service, and feasted on each other. I now know every square inch of her beautiful body intimately. But we didn't just have sex. We talked and talked and talked. About our lives. Our loves. Our passions.

This morning as we are eating breakfast on the terrace the doorbell rings.

"Did you order something else?" Katie asks me.

"Sorta," I say with a smile. "I promised to take you to the museums, remember?"

"Is that why we're here?" she teases. "I thought it was for mind-blowing sex."

"That too. Stay put. I'll be right back."

I go to the door and let Kym, who is both mine and Keatyn's stylist, into the suite. She greets me with air kisses and then moves aside so the bellmen can wheel in the racks of clothing she's brought with her. While Kym gets set up in the living room, I walk back onto the terrace.

"What's going on in there?"

"That's my stylist, Kym."

"She's Keatyn's stylist, too. I've met her before."

"That's good, because you get to go shopping without leaving our suite."

"Thank goodness!" she smirks. "I am so tired of being naked."

"Did I mention that I get to watch you try on all the clothes?" I smirk.

"DO I REALLY need a ball gown?" she asks a few minutes later as she's pursuing the racks.

"Everyone needs a ball gown in their closet," Kym replies. "You should always pack a party dress. You never know what fabulousness an invitation might lead to."

"Okay. So, pick one?"

Kym puts her hand on her hip in frustration, so Katie points at me. "Blame him! He won't tell me what we're doing."

"I am fully aware of your activities." She hands her a sleek black gown. "Go behind the rack and start with this."

I'm sitting on a low-slung couch and can see a sexy sliver of Katie naked between the clothes. I'm leaning over just a little bit more, trying to improve my view when Kym swats the back of my head. "Knox Daniels, you cad. Just because you brought me here, does not mean you get to peek. I would suggest you go make yourself busy while us girls play dress up. I want you to be surprised when you see Katie in her new clothes."

"Does that mean you're going to tell me when to wear what?" Katie asks, stepping from behind the rack. My jaw nearly drops to the floor.

"Um, I vote for that one," I say, taking in her curves barely held in place by the slinky fabric. "Anytime. Anywhere. Now, would be fine."

"Scat," Kym says, looking a little scary. She hands Katie

another gown and then rummages through her bag and hands me a stack of papers with a jewelry box underneath. "Why don't you go over these *sketches*? They are tuxedo mock-ups for your next red carpet," she lies.

I take the stack and go into the bedroom. After locking the door, so Katie won't accidentally walk in on me, I open the box. Inside are ten sparkling diamond rings of different shapes and sizes. I look at each one carefully, but my eyes are instantly drawn to one in particular. I pick it up, somehow knowing this is the one. I look at the attached tag. *Square Cut Diamond Leaf and Vine Platinum. Four carat solitaire. Five point five carat total weight.* I study the ring, the leaves curling over the top, the vines twisting up the sides. I let out a chuckle. The twisted sides remind me of her warped sense of humor for some reason. I don't bother to look at the price. It doesn't matter. This is the one.

I remove the tag and place it into the single ring box. It's perfect.

I can't fucking believe I'm doing this. But when you know it's right, you go for it.

Knox-style.

CAPTIVE FILMS—SANTA MONICA

"YOU'RE IN EARLY," I say, stopping at Riley's office before going to mine.

"Yeah, couldn't really sleep last night," he says, running his hand through his hair. It's a Johnson family gesture and means we're upset. Frustrated. Trying to figure something out.

"How come?" I take a seat in front of his desk, remembering the advice I gave him just yesterday, wondering if it was the right thing to say. If he acted on it.

"If you feel guilty, does it mean what you did was wrong?" he asks.

"That depends," Tyler says, joining us. "Did you indulge in something wonderful?"

"Yeah, I think I kind of did." He pulls a photo out of his pocket and holds it up for us. "It's . . .

"An ultrasound," I finish, pulling the photo from his hand and studying it. "It is just incredible how small the baby is but yet it's kicking and moving its little arms." I hand the photo to Tyler.

"Aww! Things like this just make me want to cry. The gift of life. I have news," he says. "Raul and I are going to adopt."

"You are?"

"Yes," he says, whipping out a photo of his own.

"It's a dog," Riley and I say at the same time.

"I know! Her name is Celine Elizabeth, and she's a York-shire Terrier. Isn't she precious? We're so thrilled." He rips the puppy photo out of Riley's hand and says, "I'm off. I have so much to do today!"

After he leaves, I hand the ultrasound photo back to Riley. "You didn't tell me you were going for an ultrasound yesterday."

"She went without me on Tuesday."

"Why didn't you go with her?"

"I was out with Ariela."

"Well, there will be other ones. Is that what you feel guilty about? Missing it?"

"Uh, no." He taps his pen on his desk absentmindedly. "I took your advice. Asked her out for dinner. When I got there, she was dressed in sexy lingerie. Anyway, she ended up straddling me and, like, I was inside of her, when she handed me the ultrasound. She said showing me that way was a bit untraditional, but that it fit our relationship. And I was just so overcome by emotion. Then she said it, and I did too."

"Said what?"

"I love you. And now I feel so guilty. For fucking her. For possibly leading her on. For not being faithful to Ariela."

"But it didn't feel wrong at the time, did it?"

"No, that's the problem. It didn't. And I don't know what the fuck that means."

"You shouldn't feel guilty, Riley. You're single."

"Yeah, but it doesn't feel like I am. I used to have no problem juggling women."

"It's different when your feelings are involved. Don't put pressure on yourself. See where those feelings lead you." He nods. "You know, I was talking to Mom yesterday. She wants to have kind of a going away party for the girls next weekend. And Whitney's fundraiser is Thursday."

"You're not letting the girls go, are you?"

"No. It's a school night, so I have an easy out. The girls are going to celebrate Halloween with their friends there, then Saturday Mom wants all of us to go to the Hamptons. She's doing an early Thanksgiving since we won't get back for it and wants you there. Any chance of that happening?"

"We'll take my plane," I suggest. "How's that sound?"

"It sounds great. And you have a birthday coming up. Any plans? Want to go back to Vegas?"

"Honestly, I forgot about my birthday. I'll let you know if I come up with some ideas."

"You should celebrate. It's the last birthday of your twenties."

"Hey, don't rub it in."

Tyler interrupts us on the intercom, reminding Riley his conference call is about to start.

"I have to go anyway," I tell him, looking at my watch.

I DON'T TELL him about Vanessa's appointment. I'm not nervous about it because I really don't think a missed period equals cancer, but she's so worried that I can't help but wonder if she knows something innately. I sure hope not.

I wanted to drive her but she said she had a client appointment this morning and figured it would keep her mind off the waiting. So I meet her there.

I give her a quick kiss and a reassuring hug and tell her everything will be okay.

We're taken into a room, spoken to briefly by a nurse, and fortunately the doctor quickly follows.

"Vanessa, it's been awhile," he says, causing her to cringe. "How are you doing?"

She doesn't bother introducing me, she just launches into it. "I think I have cancer. I know I'm supposed to come every year, but it's just so hard to see you after everything that happened. No offense."

"None taken," he says. "Why do you think you have cancer?"

She replies with the same list of reasons she gave me.

"Tell you what. I'm going to have the nurse come back in. Let's do some basic blood work and get a urine sample. I'll be back in shortly, hopefully to put your mind at ease. And we'll do a pap test and send that off to the lab."

She nods, but doesn't reply. She's a mess. Tense and on the verge of a teary meltdown. I try to rub her back, but she shrugs me off. "I can't deal right now, Dawson. Please don't touch me."

I sit back down in my spot.

And wait.

First, a nurse comes in and draws blood, then she sends Vanessa off to the restroom with a plastic cup.

I'm running prayers through my mind. Because now I'm tense too and feeling a little like Riley. Surely the universe wouldn't bring this wonderful woman back into my life, only to have her die.

When she comes back from the restroom, I can't help myself. I take my hand in hers and gently caress it. "It will all be okay. Whatever it is, I promise you and I will get through it together. I love you so much, and you make me so incredibly happy."

She gazes into my eyes, still teary, and says, "Don't talk."

"I can't talk?"

"No. I'm too worked up. Just keep holding my hand," she says, putting the death grip on it.

The doctor comes back in a long fifteen minutes later.

"Well, I have some good news," he says, setting a file down on the counter.

"I don't have ovarian cancer? Can you tell that already?"

"No, but I can tell you the cause of your missed period." He grins. "Congratulations, Vanessa, you're pregnant."

"What?! Is that some kind of sick joke?" she yells out. "How could you even say that to me after everything I've been through?"

"What do you mean?"

"You told me that I couldn't get pregnant."

"No, I told you that due to the scarring that occurred with your miscarriage it was *highly unlikely* that you would get pregnant. You beat the odds." He turns to me. "Would you be the father?"

"Uh, yeah," I reply, still trying to recover from the shock.

"Well, congratulations to both of you then."

"Wait," Vanessa says, grabbing his coat. "Are you absolutely, one-hundred percent, positively sure that I am pregnant? You didn't mix up my urine with someone else's? Because I don't believe you."

"Tell you what. Let's do it again, together." He reaches in a cabinet and pulls out another cup. "Go see if you can get us a sample and bring it back in here. We'll do the test together."

"Uh, okay," she says as she leaves.

"She seems a bit upset. Is the pregnancy unwanted?" the doctor asks me.

"She was under the impression that she couldn't get pregnant."

"When she had her miscarriage, she was understandably upset. I saw in the papers that her relationship with her husband didn't survive the ordeal."

"No, he handled it poorly. And she was devastated. She told me recently that she was hoping to adopt. She very much wants children, but she didn't expect this."

Vanessa comes back into the room. She has a haunted look in her eye—memories of her past mixed with being unable to even consider the happy news until she sees it for herself.

The doctor takes the sample from her, pulls a test out of the cabinet, and places the stick into the urine. "Of course, we'll send your blood in for a full work-up, but since you should be about five weeks along, it will show up in the urine just fine."

He sets the stick flat on the surface, and it nearly instantly turns positive. "See? You really are pregnant."

"Um, I need a minute," she says quietly, sitting down and staring at the pink line.

"Of course," he says and quickly exits.

I wait for her to say something.

But she doesn't. Tears stream down her face as she continues staring at the stick. I can't wait any longer to speak. I place my hand on her knee. "Are they happy tears?" I dare ask.

She looks up at me, like she forgot I was in the room. "I think so," she says.

The doctor comes back into the room. "Vanessa, I know you will be nervous about this one, and I don't want you stressed, so we'll monitor you closely. In fact, I was thinking maybe you should take a look now."

"Take a look?"

"Yes, let's do a quick ultrasound."

"Um, okay," she says. He hands her a robe to put on and explains to her what a transvaginal ultrasound is and how it can detect things earlier than a regular ultrasound. He steps out while she changes, and I have to ask.

"Vanessa, would I be the father?"

Her eyes get huge. "Yes, Dawson. A million times yes. You are the only person I've had sex with in a while."

I breathe a sigh of relief and nod. "Okay, good. I didn't want to be presumptuous."

"Dawson," she starts to say, but the doctor knocks and comes back in and gets everything all set up.

In a few moments we have confirmation. "See that?" the doctor says. "That circle is the yolk sac. And that there," he points," is the gestational sac. It's too early to hear or see a heartbeat. That will be at least another week or two, but you are most definitely pregnant, and everything looks completely normal."

I watch in awe.

"We're having a baby, Dawson," she whispers.

Then the doctor leaves the room with a promise to come back with prenatal vitamins and a bag full of other goodies.

She turns to me. "I'm sorry. I didn't know there was even a chance I could get pregnant."

"Yeah, I could tell." I laugh. "When you accused the doctor of making a sick joke."

"I don't expect—"

"Don't even say it," I tell her. "I couldn't be more thrilled."

"Really?" she asks. And I can tell she wants to believe me, but she still can hardly believe it's true.

"Yeah." I place my hand across her belly. "Remember that night when you told me you felt like a genie in a bottle?"

"You asked if you could rub me and make three wishes."

"Do you remember what you wished for?"

"Not really, why?"

"Because I do. I wished that you would get your wishes. That you would find big love—the kind of love that can't be torn apart, the kind of love that heals and inspires, the kind of love that lasts forever—that you could have children, and that you would be happy." I take her face in my hands and pull her into a kiss. "We're getting our wishes, Vanessa."

THE ROYAL SUITE-GEORGETOWN

A LIMO PICKS us up and drives us around to see all the significant monuments. We have tour guides take us through the Natural History Museum. Then a private tour of the White House, where I even got to meet the President.

"It's been such a fun day, Knox," I say, swinging our clasped hands in the air as we make our way back to the hotel suite.

"You look adorable in your outfit."

"I feel a little like Jackie O in this suit. It's very D.C." She leans in and gives me a kiss. "So what are we doing tonight?"

"We're going to paint the town red. First stop, the symphony at the Kennedy Center and then a cozy late-night dinner."

When we open the door to the suite, I find it looking much like my apartment did—covered with roses.

"Knox!" I screech.

He shrugs. "I had them flown here from your apartment. Didn't want them to go to waste." He plucks one of the roses from a large bouquet. "My dearest, Kathryn Katie Sugar Lips Colter, will you accept this rose from me and accompany me on a date tonight?"

I swoon. Dammit, but I do. "Of course."

There are snacks set out on the dining room table, somehow all hot, waiting for our arrival. "Thought we could have a quick bite before we leave again. The symphony starts at eight," he says, glancing at his watch. "We don't have a lot of time."

"I know exactly what I'm supposed to wear tonight, even though Kym wouldn't tell me where we were going. Get dressed and stay out here. I want to make an entrance."

He agrees and I rush into the bathroom and freshen up my makeup, doing my eyes darker than I had today. I twist my hair into a simple up-do, spritz on some perfume, and within about thirty minutes, I'm remarkably dressed and ready to go.

WHEN I MAKE my grand entrance wearing a gorgeous gown, I find Knox sitting behind the large desk talking on his phone. His dimples flash as he breaks into a wide smile upon seeing me, but his beautiful eyes are full of desire. I bask in it. Knox Daniels thinks I'm sexy. Which makes me feel like the sexiest woman alive.

As I strut over to the desk, I think about our visit to the Oval Office today. How I whispered to Knox wondering how many blowjobs have been given from underneath the Resolute Desk over the years. And how I wished I could get him behind it.

I think he would have somehow made it happen had it not been for some last minute national security update that caused us to get kicked out of the room. But seeing Knox sitting there, I can't help it.

He's still talking animatedly on the phone, and he looks like the movie star that he is in his black velvet smoking jacket. I push his chair away from the desk, then drop to my knees and slip under it. He opens his mouth and gives me a look that says *are you really going to?*

I don't even bother with an explanation. No need. I just unzip his pants, push down his boxers, and take him in my mouth.

"Uh, so, Charley, it was, uh, great talking to you, and I'll definitely consider the offer. Uh, I, need to go. I think I'm, uhhhhh, late or somethingggggg."

Based on his voice and the motions of his hips, he's clearly ready to lose it. Just a little more . . .

"Oh, fuccccckkk, gawd, that feels so good!" he finally cries out. I swallow, wipe the back of my hand across my mouth, and then push his chair back out.

"Now I feel just like the President," he says, pulling me onto his lap and straight to his lips.

SATURDAY, OCTOBER 25TH
KEATYN & AIDEN'S HOME - CHELSEA

Keatyn

WHEN WE ARRIVE in London, Aiden immediately takes me to the building he wants to remodel. It's on a beautiful street in Chelsea. The front of the building is a little tired looking, but it has great bones.

Inside, however is another story.

"This place is a wreck," I say, surveying the garbage and dust. "But the location is great."

"I know. It's going to cost a small fortune to renovate. That's why it's been empty for so long. But we've cleaned it all out and . . ."

"We? I thought you said you didn't do the deal yet?"

"I haven't. This used to be a hotel. It was stuck in a legal battle between heirs that went on for years. It was in rough shape before that, but with no care, it's gotten worse. Apparently one of the heirs now has control and is eager to close, so he agreed to pay to have it stripped to the studs so we could see what we were working with. Although, they didn't do that great of a job."

I look around at the details. "I love the high ceilings and the space. The windows are really gorgeous. It looks like maybe the floors could be refinished and the exposed brick is very cool."

"I agree." He takes my hand and leads me around, pointing. "This would be the restaurant, over here would be the wine tasting. This is the retail space. Imagine lots of dark wood, black metal, old world but with a bit of an industrial vibe. Kind of like the vineyard reception area."

"That sounds very cool. What about up there?" I ask, pointing to a surprisingly sturdy looking staircase.

"That's something I wanted to ask your advice on," he says, leading me up the stairs. "I thought we'd open up the second floor to give it a loft feel. It could be rented out for private functions or serve as overflow when we're busy. But there are three upper floors I was thinking about turning into a private club."

"An exclusive place to hang out? I love it. That's a brilliant idea, Aiden. I'm so happy for you."

"I will be purchasing the building then leasing the space back to the businesses. So I could do anything with the top three floors that I want. I could do apartments, condos. Office space."

"I like your idea of the club better. Should I ask how much?"

"It's a big undertaking, but I have a somewhat silent investor."

"Who?"

"Grandpa Douglas. He had a fair amount of Captive stock himself."

"I suppose, he put up the money to buy it originally. I've bought him out over the years, but he still holds five percent."

"He's going to help me buy the building."

"That's exciting but, you know, you could have done it yourself with *our* money."

"We haven't really talked much about what you wanted to

do with it."

"Some of it will start the new Captive. The rest I figured we'd invest. Put into a trust for our future kids." I smirk at him. "Buy a new house in London."

"Okay, so I may have already spent some of it," he grins.

"I love you," I say, sliding into his arms and kissing him. "I love your vision. Your excitement. And if you'll let me, I'd love to invest in what you're doing here."

"I was hoping you would say that."

"Why?"

"Because your grandfather says you're like Midas. Everything you touch turns to gold."

I reach down and touch my stomach. "I just want our babies to be healthy."

His hand moves to cover mine. "They will be. I'm sure of it."

"I hope so. Speaking of hope, I hope we can finally go see our new house."

He pulls me back into his arms and studies my face. "Are you sure you're okay with me taking this on? We agreed to slow down, live in Sonoma, and then I go and do this. And," he says, the corners of his mouth turning down, "if it does well, we already have investors lined up to open them in other cities around the world. New York, L.A., Dubai, Barcelona, and Miami."

"Aiden, if we have a house here, we'll be comfortable either place. I love London. And I expect our children will be traveling at a very young age. Plus, I haven't seen you this excited about something in a really long time. You're passionate about it. And your passion is one of the things I find most sexy about you. That and your smile."

"Not my body?" he teases, pushing his hips into mine.

"Well, maybe your body a little. And your gorgeous green eyes." I smirk and look behind him. "And probably that ass."

He smacks mine. "You're bad. Come on, Boots. Time for the next tour."

WE GET BACK in the car and have our driver follow the navigation to the new house.

As soon as we pull up to the modern masterpiece, Aiden starts reciting everything he knows about it.

"It's discreetly located behind secure gates, since security issues are always of concern. It's in Chelsea, so you know there is great shopping and restaurants, but also great schools, which is more important now."

"What's it made of?" I ask, noticing the dark surface covering the outside.

"Glass and black basalt mostly, with some bronze details."

"Well, I love the outside. Do we own the whole thing?"

"Yes," he says, walking me to the front door.

I notice the plaque hung over the doorbell. "Asher Place? You already named the house?"

Aiden beams. "Nope, Boots, this property has had that name for longer than you and I have been around."

"Is that why you bought it?"

"Step inside and you'll see why I bought it. The name was just proof that it was meant to be ours."

But he doesn't let me step inside, he sweeps me off my feet and carries me over the threshold. As soon as the door is shut behind us, a yellow, barking blur is jumping on us.

"Bliss! I missed you," I say as Aiden sets me down. I pick up the puppy and am rewarded with a million sweet kisses before I can actually look around.

But when I do, all I say is, "Wow, Aiden."

RILEY'S PENTHOUSE – L.A.

Riley

I LIE IN bed, looking up at the ceiling and wondering what to make of my life. Wondering what direction I should go. In business, I'm fearless and love taking calculated risks. I make decisions quickly and without remorse. Why can't I do so in my personal life?

What is it that Grandpa Douglas says? When you can't make up your mind, you should flip a coin. And that as the coin hits the ground, before you even look at it, you'll know what you want. Except even that won't work for me, because I don't know what I want.

But on my bedside table is a penny I shoved in my pocket after finding it on the floor at the club last night. The head was up, which is supposed to mean luck, and I figured I could use some of that. I shouldn't have gone to the club. All it did was further depress me, and I didn't stay long. Really, I went because I was pissed. Last night I called Ariela and asked if she wanted me to come up to Sonoma for the weekend.

She had a good reason for not wanting me to. She has meetings set up with contractors and is still working on getting her office set up. All I really heard was the word *no*.

And instead of hooking up with Shelby, I thought maybe the club would help get them both off my mind.

But it didn't.

"What the hell," I say out loud. I reach over, grab the penny, and look at it. Tails it's Shelby, because she's got an incredible ass. And heads it's Ariela, because she has the face of an angel. I throw it up and let it land on my bed, but when I do, I close my eyes. And Grandpa's right. I do see something. I see

117

Ariela's smiling face as she chased me under the pier *and* I see the ultrasound photo.

Which is basically no help. So I call Dallas.

"Hey, you wanna get in eighteen this afternoon?"

"Sure, I already have a tee time. One of the other guys just called and cancelled if you want to join us."

"That sounds great. Could I come over after that, maybe. See the baby?"

"Avoiding Ariela and the baby mama?" he says with a laugh.

"Something like that."

"You should book yourself for a massage after golf. If you're going to venture over to my place later, you're gonna need it."

DAWSON'S HOME - MALIBU

Dawson

"I KEEP THINKING yesterday was just a dream," Vanessa tells me as we're floating together in the heated pool at my house and enjoying the sun shining on our face.

"You're pregnant, Vanessa. Against all odds. Just another sign that we were meant for each other."

"M-F-E-O," she sighs happily. "I remember the first time I heard that in the movie *Sleepless in Seattle*."

"What does that mean?" I ask, confused.

"It's short for what you just said. Made for each other."

"Oh, that's cute. Sounds like something Ava and her friends would say about a boy."

"It's even cuter that you said it about me," she says, swimming over and wrapping her arms around my neck.

"I'm happy for us." I give her a sweet kiss. "It was incredible having the ultrasound so soon. That was a first for me. The baby was fully formed by the time we got to see the girls." I think back to the ultrasound that Riley showed me yesterday. How the baby was so much more developed than what I just saw in ours. I'm trying to figure out how much further along Shelby would be when Vanessa interrupts my thoughts.

"Tyler told me that the fundraiser for your, for Whitney, is coming up."

"Yes, it's next Thursday. I'll be going back home anyway to help pack up for our move. I wanted to talk to you about that. Do you remember how I invited you to come home with me for Thanksgiving?"

"I remember that I wasn't sure we'd even be together that long. Now look at us. You're moving in with your girls. We're going to be a family."

"Well, I hate to do it," I say with a smirk, "but I'm going to have to rescind that offer."

"But why?"

"Because we won't be going home for Thanksgiving. My mom decided to throw the girls a big going away party and combine that with our traditional Thanksgiving dinner. So I'm hoping you can come with me next weekend. The girls want you to meet everyone. As do I."

"I'd love that. Do you want me to go to the fundraiser with you, too?" I let out a sudden breath at the thought of her having to deal with Mrs. Clarke. She sees my reaction and immediately says, "Oh, I don't have to. I don't want it to be awkward for you."

"No, it's not that at all. Whitney's mother is horrible. I told her neither the girls nor I could come, that I was busy with my new job. I guess she moved the date to this coming week and with me being in town, which she's sure to hear about from the girls, I really do have to go. And while I'd love for you to go and help me get through it, I wouldn't wish that on you."

"Do you think she would be mean or something?"

"Absolutely. If she knows that we're moving in with you, she will be horrified that we're living in sin or something. She'll threaten to sue me for custody. She'll accuse me of having an affair with you while I was married. It's really hard to say what she would come up with, but it won't be pretty or remotely nice."

"I think I could handle it," she says confidently. "If you want my support, I'll be there."

"I appreciate it."

"Do you think it's setting a bad example for the girls for us to be moving in together, to be having a baby together and not be married? Or would it be a worse example to be getting married after only knowing each other for like a month. I mean, not that I'm suggesting we get married. . . " she dunks her head down under the water, apparently feeling stressed.

When she comes up, my mouth finds hers. "God, you're beautiful."

"I'm all wet," she scoffs.

"Exactly." I pick her up and carry her to the hot tub, where I pull her onto my lap after slipping off her bikini bottoms.

THE ROYAL SUITE-GEORGETOWN
Knox

"I DON'T WANT to get out of bed, Knox," Katie whines, even though it's late afternoon. Not that I really want to leave this room either, but there's something important I have to do tonight.

Propose.

Part of me thinks I'm out of my mind for doing this. All the time, energy, money, and preparation that went into planning tonight is ridiculous, and I'll be truly crushed if she says no. But I take solace in the fact that she told me she would have said yes if I would have proposed on the school steps. It's hard to believe that was only a few days ago.

I know her so much better now. And the more I know, the harder I fall. Her body is my perfection. Her heart is kind and caring. Her voice is like the flutter of an angel's wings. Her scent completely intoxicating. Her wit daring.

"It's our one week anniversary, sugar. We must celebrate the end of my bachelor journey."

"The end?" She furrows her adorable brow.

"Yes. The weekend is coming to a close."

"Back to reality, I guess." She gets out of bed, grabs her robe from the floor, and throws it around herself in a huff.

Not exactly the reaction I was looking for. She watches the show, shouldn't she be excited about what happens at the end? Or did she not mean what she said?

When Katie disappears into the bathroom, and I hear the shower turn on, I race into the living room and call Missy.

"Am I completely bat-shit crazy for doing this?" is the first thing out of my mouth when she answers.

"Of course, you are. But isn't that what love is all about? If it isn't crazy, reckless, and passionate, it's not worth it. Love shouldn't be ordinary. It should be extraordinary. And it's quite clear that you feel that way about Katie. She's going to be shocked tonight. She's going to cry. She's going to wonder what the hell is going on, but she's going to love it. Because your love for her is so apparent. And after tonight, if she had any doubts, those will be put completely to rest."

"You think it will all go smoothly? Like we planned?"

"That's why you brought me along for the ride, Knox. To make sure of it."

I let out a sigh of relief. "You're right."

"And remember, if it doesn't, just go with it. Improvise. You're an actor. And be careful with the explosion. You know I hate when you do your own stunts."

"Ha. That's the least of my worries! You know the combination for the safe. You'll have everything ready here when we get back?"

"Yes, I will. And let me guess, it's the four digit code you always use. 8008. Looks like it spells boob. Well, at least your hopefully-future bride fits your anatomical wish list."

"That she does."

I hang up feeling better about tonight. The shower is still on, so I decide to join her, but when I get outside the door, I think I hear crying.

I fling open the door to find Katie sitting on the bench crying.

"What's the matter?" I jump into the shower with her, immediately soaking my robe.

"You weren't supposed to hear me," she sniffles.

"Why are you crying, Katie?" I reach out and smooth her wet hair out of her eyes.

"Because tonight's . . . the end."

"You don't want to leave Washington?"

"I don't want to leave you!" she yells then starts sobbing again.

"But why would you? You said you'd move in with me. Did you not mean it?"

She stops crying and stares at me wide-eyed. "I didn't know if you meant it, Knox. When you just said this was the end—I don't know—it just made me very sad."

I grab her face and kiss her. "I don't want you to be sad. I'm sorry we haven't discussed the details. I've been having so much fun just being with you here and now, I kind of forgot about the real world."

"How do you picture us in the real world?"

"Together. Forever."

A smile blazes across her face. "You're crazy. Seriously. Logistically, how is this even going to work? Aren't you and Keatyn filming on location soon?"

"We are. We'll be in London for about a month, then a whirlwind of other places—Dubai, Paris. I forget where else. Will you come with me?"

"Knox, as much as I'd love to, I can't just quit my job on a whim. I mean, no offense, but I read the tabloids. And I know not all of it is true, but . . ."

Shit. I can't ruin the surprise. I don't want to just fucking propose right here. No, improvise. What can I say to placate her for now? "You told me our kiss was life-changing. It doesn't matter what has happened in my life up until this point, because you have altered it. I want to be with you, Katie. All the time. I guess I just assumed you'd want to go with me."

"To London?"

"Yes. I'll be there for a month, staying at Keatyn and Aiden's new place. Hopefully, with you."

"And then what?"

"A few other locations."

"And would I stay in London while you're gone?"

"That's up to you. When we are on location our days are really long which means you'd be alone a lot. I mean, you could come on set if you wanted, but trust me after a few days it gets a little boring. I thought you could talk to Keatyn about it, and she might be able to help you decide."

She's nodding, which I hope is a good sign, and the tears seem to have dried up.

"It's scary, you know. Like just quitting your job and taking that risk. I don't have your kind of bank account to fall back on if it doesn't work out."

"Could you get a leave of absence? Would that make you

feel more comfortable?"

"Yeah, maybe," she says. "Actually, that would make me feel better. Like until I know we're fully committed."

I want to tell her in a few days, if she agrees, we'll be fully committed, but I don't.

"So, is everything okay now? Do you still want to go on our date?"

"You spent a lot of time planning this weekend, didn't you?" she asks, running her hand down my arm. I try not to immediately stiffen, because we don't have a lot of time for shower fun.

"I did," I tell her, glancing down at my dick. "And as much as I want to take you in this shower, we don't have much time before we have to leave."

"Are we on a schedule?"

"Yeah, sugar, we are."

THE ROYAL SUITE–GEORGETOWN

As KNOX AND I step outside of the hotel to our waiting limousine, I don't feel like I'm on the arm of a movie star. I feel like *I'm* the movie star. The way Knox looked at the dress I'm wearing literally made me blush—and I am not the least bit bashful. Especially since he has seen every single intimate part of me over the course of the last few days. I'm nervous. I love the whole *Bachelor* theme of this weekend, but I can't quite figure out what tonight is about. If I were really on the show and had made it to the final round, tonight would be the night I would find out if I had won his heart or if I was going home in tears.

It's the going home in tears part that has me worried. He seemed upset that I was crying in the shower. He seems sincere in wanting me to move in with him, but it's like I'm living a dream, and I keep waiting to wake up—wondering when it will be over.

But I can't live that way. I never have. So, I'm going to put on a smile, flirt and kiss the sexy-as-hell man sitting next to me, and enjoy the moment.

SOON THE LIMO is pulling to a stop. When Knox helps me out of the car, I'm shocked to find us at a harbor.

I'm ready to ask why when he takes my hand and leads me down to the docks, where there is a yacht waiting for us.

"Knox Daniels," I say. "I swear you must have a team of planners hidden away somewhere."

"Just my assistant, Missy, who has watched the show from the beginning."

"I'd like to meet her."

"You will later."

"Ahoy, I'm Captain Michaels," a tall man in a captain's hat says. "Welcome aboard."

We're offered champagne and then led out to a deck where a table for two is set for dinner.

Knox pulls out my chair, and I take a seat. Then he holds his glass up. "Everything that happens tonight is because of you. You inspire me. Cheers."

"Cheers," I reply, wondering what exactly he means.

But nothing really seems to happen. We enjoy a lovely dinner while we cruise down the Potomac river, passing by the Jefferson Memorial, the Washington Monument, the John F. Kennedy Center, and the Memorial Bridge. The lights are beautiful, and I enjoy seeing the city from this vantage point.

And when it starts misting a little and I ask if we can go inside, he looks at his watch and says, "Not just yet."

Instead, he produces an umbrella and pours me another glass of champagne.

SOON AFTER, WE'RE joined on the deck by—and you're never going to believe it—the actual host of the television show.

"It's time for the ceremony to begin," he says, while Knox gives me a wickedly adorable grin. "Please come with me."

He leads me into the main salon, which looks like an actual television set. There are men with cameras and microphones and all sorts of stuff to make this all look—and feel—real. I see a podium with a single red rose lying on it. I'm taken past it to one of the boat's bedroom suites. This one featuring a huge television screen.

"You'll be watching the interviews live," he says. "Wait here until you're called."

I sit on the edge of the bed, feeling like I'm at home watching one of my favorite shows. Except Knox comes on the screen and sits down.

"So, Knox," the host says. "Tell us how you are feeling about your journey so far."

Knox looks straight into the camera, or maybe it's just the angle, but I swear it's like he's speaking just to me.

"I came here to find love. And from the start, one girl captured my heart. It's a little scary, really, opening your heart to love. But I can honestly say that I've found it. The girl I want to spend the rest of my life with."

Next the screen flashes to a woman. She's about forty, has short dark hair, gorgeous skin, and a beautiful smile. She's wearing a long gown like I am, but it's more modestly cut.

"So, Missy," the host says, "Are you ready for whatever happens tonight?"

"Of course. I am sure of the love I share with Knox and I am sure that I will receive the final rose tonight." She turns and winks at the camera. I don't know who this is, but she's a hoot.

Pretty. Funny. I like her already. Except for the part about her saying she loves Knox.

Then it's just her on the screen.

I wonder what in the world is going on. On the show, the other contestant never gets to watch this. But this lady is funny. She's being interviewed and going on and on about Knox.

"Really, the other girls didn't stand a chance. From the moment Knox and I met, to our first kiss, to the fantasy suite where we did nothing but talk all night—" She gives the camera another wink. "Our love has been apparent to everyone around us. And that night in the fantasy suite, well it's where we really, uh, first connected. And I know without a doubt when this ceremony ends tonight, he will be down on one knee, presenting me with a ring." Then she whispers, "That bitch Katie doesn't stand a chance."

A few moments later, she's joining Knox out in the salon, where the single rose is on display. She rushes into his arms, gives him an exaggerated kiss on the cheek, tells him she loves him, and then holds his hands.

I'm trying to figure out who the hell she is but then he says, "Hello, Missy."

Wait, didn't he say that was the name of his assistant? Oh my gosh, I love her. She's freaking hilarious and is so having fun. I want to be her best friend.

"Knox," she says, flashing him an overly sexy smile. "You made me feel like taking a chance on love again. My heart is overflowing with love for you, and I can't wait to share a life together."

As typical on the show, the bachelor stands there and listens and tries not to give anything away.

"I have to admit, I never thought I would find love on a show like this, and competing against all these other girls was so difficult when all I wanted to do was be with you, but it was worth it. I'll forever be grateful to the heavens above for aligning our stars. I love you, Knox. More than anything in the world."

She flips her hair and lowers her shoulder, allowing him a clear shot of her ample cleavage. Then she winks at him.

Knox looks into her eyes and says, "I didn't know what to expect out of all of this. Would I find love? Would I find the one or would this just be a great vacation where I'd get to make out with a lot of hot girls? But I fell in love. We fell in love, and I love you, I do." He sighs. "But . . . ."

After a dramatic pause, Knox is replaced on the screen by a commercial break consisting of two ads. Both featuring Knox. One for watches that I have actually seen on television before and another a hilarious one for insurance where he plays multiple different roles.

I'm practically rolling on the ground laughing by the time it ends.

Then he and Missy come back on.

"But, Missy. I don't love you the most."

Her eyes get big, and her mouth drops open. "What?!" she yells. "You what? You told me you loved me. Did you tell everyone that?!"

"Um, no, not exactly," Knox says, rubbing her shoulder and trying to keep her from having a meltdown. "I meant what I said. I do love you. I always will, but you're not the one for me. I'm sorry."

"You know what, Knox Daniels?" she screams, shaking her finger at his face. "That's total and complete bullshit! What about the fantasy suite? All the things we said and *did*?"

"That was part of getting to know you, Missy."

"Well, you got to know me in the biblical sense, Knox!" Then she breaks down and starts crying, falling dramatically to the ground. "They were all lies!"

Knox helps her up then takes her out to a waiting limo and shuts her inside.

"That was rough," he says, as the limo pulls away.

Then a camera feed from the inside of the limo shows her sobbing. "I will never love again. Ever!" she screeches. "Unless I get my own show." She looks at the camera and winks again.

The door to my room opens and a makeup artist comes in. She shines a spotlight on me, powders my nose, and runs a product through my hair that makes it look gorgeously silky smooth.

When she's finished, she says, "You're up."

I take a deep breath, open the door, and join Knox in the salon. I mean, the other girl is gone, so I know I'm the one. I know I will get the final rose. And I think it's really sweet that he went through all this trouble to recreate the show just for me.

I know that if we're following the format of the show close-ly, I'm supposed to tell him how I feel first, so I'm trying to come up with the right words when he takes my hands in his and says, "I've dated a lot in my life. I've loved before. But the *right* one was elusive. I wondered if I was unlovable, if I had too big of an ego, if was I too picky, too critical, or not ready. I wondered if it truly was my problem, not theirs. But with one simple, wonderfully naughty question, you changed all that. You made me realize it wasn't me. That not finding the one in the past meant that I ended up in that spot meeting you at that exact moment in my life. And when we kissed, sugar," he says with a smile so big he almost has two dimples in each cheek, "for the first time in my life I understood the saying about going weak in the knees. Your kiss opened my heart, touched my soul, and literally has brought me to my knee. One knee."

My eyes get big—because *one knee*?

He takes a deep breath and gets down on one knee.

"Katie, will you marry me?"

"Ohmigawd! Are you for real?" I ask, covering my mouth with my hand. I know this is all supposed to be in fun, but a fake proposal, really?

Knox pats his suit jacket pocket, grimaces, then starts patting down all his pockets, trying to find something.

"Oh my God. The ring is gone!" he yells out. "Missy! Do you take the ring?"

"I didn't take the ring!" she yells, from somewhere not too far away. "I'm not *that* desperate, you asshole!"

The big screen in the room suddenly flashes to life and the bad guy from the last *Trinity* movie starts speaking. "I have the ring," he says, flashing it. "Not that it matters, you won't be around long enough to retrieve it." He laughs maniacally as a menacing score plays. The bad guy shows us a photo of a large bomb with a timer counting down. "You have about ten seconds, and then you won't need to get married!" He grins, holding up a detonator. "You'll be together forever, in HELL!"

Knox turns to me, his eyes wide, and grabs my arm. "We have to get out of here before it explodes!" As he drags me in my five-inch heels through the salon and up a set of stairs, he's yelling into his cuff. "Fire up the chopper!"

We get to the top of the stairs and find a military-style helicopter with its blades spinning.

"Hurry," the pilot says, as Knox pushes me inside.

"Take off! Take off," Knox screams over the loud sound of the rotors. "Or we're all dead!"

We've barely gotten out of the way when there's a large boom. I'm worried about the other people on the boat for a second, because this all seems very real. But then fireworks explode into the sky off the yacht.

Knox wipes his brow and grins at me. "Whew. That was a little too close. We barely made it."

"You, know, Knox Daniels, you are officially crazy. What are we going to do next? Land on the White House lawn?"

"No, he doesn't want the president. He wants me," Knox says, staying in character. "We're going to have to go after him. What he doesn't know is that I put a tracking device in the ring, so I'd always know where to find you."

"That's kind of romantic," I tell him, because in a weird, non-stalkerish way, it kind of is. I lean over and give him a quick peck.

"Guys, have you honed in on the tracking device yet?" he asks the pilots.

"Of, course, sir," the co-pilot says. "We're headed that way. We've got a good lock on him." Someone from behind us hands Knox a very real looking black pistol. And I realize that this helicopter is quite large and there is what appears to be a whole troop of commandos in the seats behind us.

Knox studies the gun, shoves the clip in, and says to me, "I'll get your ring back if it's the last thing I do."

"But can't we buy a new ring?" I ask. This is the point, seriously, in some of his and Keatyn's movies where I'm like, really? Do you really need to risk your life over something like this?

But then he takes my hand and kisses my ring finger. "You don't understand, sugar. This ring symbolizes everything. The start of our new life together. Away from all this. And when this is over, mark my words, we're going to be back in the fantasy suite, where I'm going to put that ring on your finger and make sweet love to you. I love you, Katie."

It's the first time he's said those words to me, and they take my breath away.

"I love you, too." I tell him.

He leans over and gives me a deep kiss. His heady scent makes me almost forget we're in a helicopter going who knows where chasing this ring. I don't even know if there really is a ring for me. Or if it will be another prop. But when he's kissing me, I don't care. Because the way he looked into my eyes when he said those three little words told me all I needed to know. He meant it.

And so did I.

Next thing I know, we are landing at some abandoned

warehouse. It's dark, decrepit, and scary looking. The kind of place where you know bad things are going to happen and should avoid at all costs.

"He's in there," Knox says valiantly. "I'm going to end this once and for all."

"We're going with you, sir," the men on the helicopter say, holding their automatic weapons up in the air. They are all decked out in full military garb, flack jackets, camouflage, helmets. I almost feel like he's really fighting for me—trying to get back the ring that will mean so much—and armed with nothing more than a pistol and really great fitting suit.

"You stay here," he says, planting a kiss on my forehead. "I'll be back before you know it."

All of the men, with the exception of the pilot, get out of the helicopter.

"Katie!" Knox yells from the street. "I love you!" Then he comes rushing back toward me, and I fling myself at him like he really is going off to battle. We share an epic, heart-felt kiss.

Then he's gone and entering the warehouse.

I'm watching the door, wondering what else will happen when I hear the *pfft pfft* sound of a silenced handgun and the pilot in front of me slumps over.

The bad guy waves a gun in my direction. "Get out of the chopper."

I'm really not sure what I'm supposed to do. I stall, waiting for Knox to burst out of the building and *save* me, but he doesn't, so I reluctantly get out. I look at the pilot and see red pouring from his head wound. Fake blood, I know, but it all looks very real—feels very real.

The bad guy pulls me into a limo and then hits me over the head with the gun in his hand. It shocks me, but then I realize the gun was made of foam.

"I just knocked you out," he whispers, "keep your eyes closed and don't open them until you're told to."

I play along wondering what the hell is going to happen next. Because I fucking can't wait.

I'm carried by two people for a short distance and then laid on a chaise. A voice comes over a speaker that says, "You've been hit over the head and are unconscious. This is a dream scene. Slowly open your eyes."

When I do, I'm shocked. I'm on a set that looks like a tropical paradise. There's an ocean and sand in front of me. Sand under my chair. Even a breeze blowing back my hair.

A moment later, a shirtless and nearly pantless Knox appears, presenting me a tropical drink on a silver tray. He's wearing what could best be described as a loin cloth. He looks so freaking sexy, I actually wonder if I am dreaming. Because, come on, it's Knox. His muscles are ripped. His skin pulled taut across thick abs. His outrageous V-line dips down into the cloth and I know exactly what kind of pleasure hides behind it.

"This is a really good dream," I mutter, taking the drink. I put my lips to the straw and am surprised to find an actual frozen piña colada.

Knox reveals his naked ass when he picks up a large palm leaf that he fans me with.

Then he sits down next to me and kisses me. And I don't know who all is watching, but I really don't care. I kiss him hard back, shoving my tongue into his mouth. Because who the hell does something like this for a girl? This is way beyond recreating some show.

"Knox-style," I mutter.

"What's that, sugar lips?" he asks.

"I said Knox-style. I didn't know what that meant until just now." I slide my hand under his loin cloth, surprised to find my hand connecting with bare skin.

"Oh, sugar," he moans, then he whispers, "Close your eyes again. The dream is almost over."

A FEW MINUTES later, I open my eyes. The dream set has changed back to the abandoned warehouse.

When the bad guy sees me looking around, he yells at me. "I have everything now. *You* and your precious ring. Trinity took *everything* from me. And now I'm going to take away everything he holds dear. We will be married. And I can't wait to celebrate our honeymoon." The bad guy shocks me with a very unwanted kiss. Like his tongue is out of his mouth and in mine before our lips even touch. And I don't want to be kissed by him, so I push him away then slap him across the face.

He takes a step back and smirks. "Like it rough, do you?" Then he slaps my face. Only he doesn't really slap me. His hand whooshes by and hits his other hand making the noise.

Then he lifts me up and brings me to his lips again.

"Let her go, Dremel," Knox yells, descending from a black rope above us, back in his suit and holding out the gun.

The bad guys pulls me closer, shoves the gun against my head, and then licks up the side of my face. "Oh no, pretty boy. She's mine now."

"The place is surrounded, Dremel. You can't escape this time."

"Oh, but I can," he replies and suddenly the floor from underneath us gives away. I scream as we fall through a trap door and land in a heap on an inflated stunt bag. My tight gown gives away on the side, ripping. I touch my hair, realizing that my up-do has half fallen out and that there are black marks on my arms from the bad guy holding me.

The trap door above us shuts, and I hear Knox cry out. A makeup artist appears out of nowhere and tells me to hurry and get up, then she powders my nose and adds gloss to my lips. "Go!"

The bad guy grabs me and now we're running up stairs. He's going too fast, and it causes me to lose one of my heels. "I lost my shoe," I tell him, but he doesn't stop.

"No time," he says, still dragging me up the stairs. When we get to the top, he runs straight into Knox's fist.

I'm pushed aside while they fight.

"It's just you and me now," Knox says.

"And when I break your neck, I'm going to celebrate between your girlfriend's legs."

"She's my fiancee," Knox yells back, jabbing him in the face.

"She doesn't have a ring yet," the bad guy chuckles, then sweeps Knox's legs out from under him.

They roll on the ground, wrestling.

And their fighting actually looks real. Knox is taking actual punches, I think, or maybe it's just good choreography. I really can't tell even from this close.

After a few minutes, Knox pushes the bad guy down the steps, runs to a *Bachelor*-type podium, grabs a rose and a ring box, rushes over to me, takes my hand, and pulls me out of the warehouse.

He stops, hits a button on a detonator that looks much like the one the bad guy had earlier, and says, "Burn in hell, mother fucker!"

Then there is an honest to God blast. Flames shoot up the front of the building, and Knox throws himself on top of me, knocking me to the ground.

I want to yell at him *what the fuck* was that, but he lifts his head from my chest and looks into my eyes as his dimples flash.

Then he leans in and gives me an epic, movie-ending kiss.

Except.

It's not the end.

"Not so fast, there," he says. "I promised you the suite." Then he picks me up and carries me to a waiting limo.

And I'm hoping there won't be any cameras there.

A SHORT TIME later, we arrive back at the hotel. I can see myself in the mirror as we enter. Makeup still perfect, dress a mess, hair a disaster, but I feel incredibly, unbelievably sexy.

Knox leads me out to the terrace, which is filled with thousands of red roses and as many hurricane lanterns flickering light.

"Let's try this again," he says. This time when he pats his jacket pocket he smiles and pulls out a box. He opens it revealing a gorgeous ring.

"Oh my God. Is any of this real?"

"I'm definitely real, sugar. And so's the rock. So, what's your answer?"

I wrap my arms around his neck. When I see myself reflecting in the depth of eyes filled with love and sincerity, I realize he's not fucking around.

He's serious.

And it takes my breath away. "Yes, Knox. Yes."

He kisses me then pulls out the rose. "Katie, will you accept my final rose?"

"Yes, give me that thing," I say with a laugh as cheesy, but perfect, romantic music starts playing.

"You're crazy. I love you," I tell him. Then we kiss. A lot.

"Is this really my ring?" I ask, looking down at it. "It's so beautiful I wonder if it's just a prop."

"It's your ring if you like it. I thought it looked like you."

"The ring looked like me?" I ask.

"Yes. You're fun, your laughter is infectious, you're playful and sweet, but you have a wonderfully naughty side. A wicked sense of humor and a dirty mind. Two things I appreciate in a woman. But, mostly, every time I think of you, you make me smile. I was drawn to this ring like I was drawn to you. It was instant—immediate. And I trust my judgment and instinct. I want very much to marry you, Katie "Bite Me" Colter."

I get goosebumps as he slips the ring on my finger.

"Oh wow," I say, staring down at the massive, glittering

stone.

"Wow?" he says, looking offended. "The ring got the same response as the first time I, uh, bit you."

"It's almost as good," I tease.

"Oh, I can't stand for that. I'm going to have to do better this time. Would you go into the fantasy suite with me now?"

"No cameras?"

"*Definitely* no cameras."

"I thought you'd never ask," I say as he picks me up, carries me into the bedroom, and throws me on the bed.

SUNDAY, OCTOBER 26TH
THE ROYAL SUITE-GEORGETOWN

Knox

AT FOUR IN the morning, we order room service, because, well, we're starved. Last night went even better than I hoped, from Missy's crazy performance—who knew she could act—to the helicopter and explosions, to when she said yes. The look on her face was priceless because I could tell she was wondering if it was all real. The best part though was when we triumphantly returned to our suite, and I gave her the ring and the rose.

It was like my life fell completely into place in that single moment.

But I want more.

Katie is naked, just the way I like her, sitting up in bed, half covered with a sheet, shoveling eggs into her mouth. "God, this tastes so good. I guess you worked up an appetite in me." She grins and waggles her eyebrows. "In more ways that one."

I lean against her, holding up her hand and staring at the ring on her finger. "It looks perfect on you. I'm so glad you like it."

"Like it? Knox, I love it." She grins again. "Although not as much as your signature move."

"You're such a liar," I say, kissing my way up her neck.

She lets out a contented sigh. "I swear I could be happy like this for the rest of my life."

"I say we do it then."

"Do what?"

"Start the rest of our life."

"I don't get it," she says, looking confused.

"Let's get married. Now."

She sets her plate on the side table and turns to me. "Married? Now? We just got engaged."

"You know how yesterday you were worried about the commitment?"

She lowers her head slightly. "I'm sorry, Knox. I was just freaking out. The thought of quitting my job on a whim for love scared me. Especially since we hadn't really talked commitment." She holds up her hand and flashes the sparkle. "But now we are, so it's okay."

"Yeah, but what I couldn't tell you last night, since we weren't engaged yet, is that I want us to elope."

"Elope?" She narrows her eyes at me. "Wait, you planned for us to elope? Are there going to be more helicopters and explosions? Are we getting married Knox-style?"

I can't help but chuckle. "No, but Kym did make sure one of the dresses you chose was white, didn't she?"

She playfully smacks my arm. "Knox Daniels, you *literally* planned all of this out, didn't you?"

"I did. I was being very literal when I said that your kiss deeply affected me."

"So in that case, where did you plan for us to elope to?"

"London."

"Why London?" she asks, cocking her head to the left, something I've noticed she tends to do when she asks a question.

"Well, we need some witnesses, and I prefer they not be strangers. Keatyn and Aiden arrived in London yesterday. I'd like them to stand up for us if you're okay with that."

"But they're on their honeymoon!"

"That's the other reason I want to do it now. We can get married and go on a fabulous honeymoon before I have to start work."

"Do you have our honeymoon planned, too?"

"I have an idea."

"Like where?"

"Positano, Italy."

"I've never been to Italy," she says.

"Actually, neither have I. And I've always wanted to go."

"Let's go there then!" She throws her arms around my neck. "I love you, Knox."

I kiss her. "I love you too, my future bride."

She visibly swoons. "Ahhh, that sounds so amazing. You're amazing."

"We're amazing," I tell her. "So does that mean yes to eloping?"

She jumps up and does a little clap, her boobs wonderfully bobbing in front of me. "Yes!" she says as I lean down to take one of her nipples in my mouth.

"Knox!" she screeches, pushing me back. "When is this elopement supposed to take place?"

"Tomorrow. Which means as soon as I can get you out of this bed, we need to fly over there. Let's call the new Mr. and Mrs. Arrington and see if they are cool with it."

"No!" she screeches, getting even more excited. "Let's FaceTime them, so I can show her my ring!" I slide the sheet down across her exquisite form.

"Well, you better put a robe on then, sugar lips."

She looks down. "Shit! I forgot I was naked. Seems like naked is all I've been since we got here!"

"And that's exactly the way I like you," I tease, pinning her to the bed. "Plus, now that my appetite for food has been suppressed, I'm hungry for you again."

"Oh, Knox," she says, pushing her hips against me. "Can we call first? I've been dying to tell someone about all this."

That makes me happy. So I jump up and grab two robes from the bathroom and catch a glimpse of myself in the mirror. At the smile plastered on my face. Have I ever felt this happy in my life? Definitely not.

I toss her a robe, pull mine on, then join her on the bed.

She glances at the clock. "Knox, is it too early to call?"

"I'm sure they will be awake by now." I press Keatyn's number for a FaceTime call. Katie has already assumed the position, her hand held up, palm facing inward to show off the rock.

"Hey, Knox," Keatyn answers. She looks like she hasn't been awake long. But then her eyes seem to adjust or maybe the picture finally makes its way to her. "Oh my God!" she screams. "Congratulations! Look Aiden, Knox and Katie got engaged!"

Aiden's face comes on the screen. He's shirtless and leaning against a padded headboard. Definitely still in bed.

"We're thinking of crossing the pond today," I say. "You up for some company at that beautiful new house of yours?"

"Well, it is our honeymoon," Aiden says warily.

"We'd like to start our honeymoon there, too."

"Wait, what?" Keatyn scrunches up her nose in confusion as their puppy, Bliss, bounds onto the bed and licks her face. "You got married without us?!"

"No, that's why we want to come there. We're eloping in London tomorrow, and we want you two to stand up for us."

"Oh my God! Yes! Yes. Of course. Katie! Tell me about the proposal."

"We'll bring the video," I say with a smirk and Katie goes, "There's a video?"

"Well, then hurry up already!" Keatyn screeches. Her excitement is palpable, and it makes me happy. I was sort of worried that she'd tell us that we are fucking nuts for wanting to get married right away.

"Aiden" I ask, with more vulnerability in my voice than I intend. "You cool with it?"

"Hey, you took my advice. I can't very well turn you down now," he teases, but I'm so touched he would allow us to interrupt their honeymoon for this. "Seriously. Congratulations. We can't wait for you to get here. Is there anything you need us to do?"

"Actually, yes," I tell him. "We want to get married tomorrow afternoon at the Chelsea Register Office, but Missy said we might have a little snag in our plan."

"What's that?"

"In order to get a marriage license we are supposed to have applied for it like a month ago. Any chance you could call your pal, the prince, and see if he could help us with that? We'll be living there during filming so we'll be in residence for a good thirty days after, if that helps."

"Yeah," Aiden says with a laugh. "I think we can do that. See you soon."

Keatyn's wide grin takes up most of the screen as she ends the call.

"What advice?" Katie asks.

"It's embarrassing," I tell her, picking up a lukewarm french fry, dipping it in the ranch dressing that she loves, and feeding it to her.

"I swear," she says, chewing. "The food I have had here has been the best of my life." She smiles. "It must be the company, not the food. And, tell me."

I snuggle up next to her, lying my head on her chest and letting my fingers trail down her body. "I knew the minute I kissed you."

"So did I," she says, arching her back slightly as I work my way down to her sweet spot.

"Which made me wonder if I was desperate."

"What?" she laughs. "You're Knox Daniels. You could get any woman you wanted. Honestly, I'm still not sure why you'd want me, but I'm going to enjoy the hell out of it while it lasts."

"That's why I want you so desperately," I tell her, sitting up and looking into her eyes, as I run my fingers through her messy hair. "Because you're fun. Because you're sexy. Because you had the kind of morals that left me standing alone on the dance floor. Because I didn't believe it could happen to me."

"Love at first sight?"

"Yes, but then I freaked out a little when I realized we had met before."

"When we were like twelve," she teases.

"I was twenty. It's hard sometimes living around people with epic love stories when you don't have one yourself."

"I feel you on that. Being single has it perks, but it also sucks sometimes."

"Exactly, and I wanted to make sure I didn't want a relationship like that so badly that I was trying to fabricate one."

"What did Aiden say?"

"He told me that I'm lucky to have met someone who made me feel that way when my heart was ready for it. And not to fuck it up."

"Well, thank goodness you didn't listen," she says, wrapping her arms around my neck and pulling me in close. "Because you have clearly been fucking me up all weekend."

"You make me laugh, Katie. Seriously. I'm so excited to marry you."

"Why don't you fuck me up a little more, then we can pack and get our asses to London."

"I need to make one more phone call. Then I'll take you up on that." She gives me a little pout, but nods.

"Riley, my man," I say when he answers.

"Knox, where the hell are you? I called to see if you wanted to go out, and you never called me back."

"You at the club now?"

"No. I'm home."

"Why? It's still early. Oh, wait. Do you have Ariela in bed with you?"

"No, definitely not. She's decided she wants to wait to have sex with me again until I agree to be monogamous."

"So you're still fucking the baby mama?"

"Sometimes."

"She there now?"

"No, I am currently alone. And damn happy about it. It's been a tricky week. So, what the fuck did you call for?"

"Hang on and I'll FaceTime you. You decent?"

"You woke me up. I sleep naked."

"Well, cover that shit up. Then you should hop in that pretty little jet of yours and hightail it to London."

He rubs his eyes. "What's in London?"

"A wedding."

"Whose?" he asks.

I pan the camera over to Katie, who flashes her ring.

Riley sits up straight in his bed. "Katie is getting married?" His eyes search the screen. "Who is Katie marrying?"

"Me," I say proudly. "Monday afternoon. In London."

"You've got to be fucking kidding me! That's awesome!"

"Does that mean you'll come?" I almost get choked up. "It would mean a lot to me."

"I'm on my way, bro. Where are we staying?"

"We're crashing Aiden's swanky new pad."

"But it's their honeymoon!"

"Yeah, well they decided we could interrupt it for this."

Riley is still shaking his head in disbelief. Actually, so I am. I don't know how I got so lucky. "I didn't even know you knew each other. Or were, like, dating. This is crazy."

"Crazy, sexy, and wonderful. We met at the wedding. I

guess it was fate—or something."

"Or *something*," Katie whispers in my ear.

"Well, congrats! I'll call the pilot and head that way!"

I hang up, feeling happy, and hug the woman who's made me that way.

"Now, back to fucking you up," I say, reaching for her.

RILEY'S PENTHOUSE - L.A.

I'M THROWING CLOTHES in my suitcase when I realize I'm not the only one who needs to be there. I give Dallas a call.

"This better be good," he says groggily.

"Knox is eloping. We need to be there."

"Where is there, exactly?"

"London. Throw some shit in a bag and meet me at the airport. We need to throw him a bachelor party."

"Hmm, let me check with the missus." I hear him speaking to RiAnne. "Hey, pookiebear, I need to go to London with Riley. You cool with that?"

"What time is it? And why is Riley calling in the middle of the night?"

"Because we need to leave, like, now."

"What are you two up to?" she wisely asks him. RiAnne has always had his number.

"Apparently Knox and Katie just got engaged and are eloping in London," Dallas says. "Riley called to see if I wanted to be there."

"And you said *hell yes*, you want to be there, right?" she asks.

"No, I told him I needed to ask you if I could go," he says

with a laugh.

"After all these years, it's finally payback time," she says, sounding a little like a movie villain seeking revenge. "It's Knox's fault you and your groomsmen were so hungover the day of our wedding. Hell, I'm pretty sure you were all *still* drunk from the night before!"

"I know I was," Dallas chuckles.

"Oh," RiAnne says, apparently grabbing the phone and talking to me. "Riley, your birthday is Tuesday. How are you celebrating? Do you want Dallas to stay and party with you?"

"That would be really nice—" I start to say.

"Well, if you want him to do that, you will help him get Knox hammered. Do you understand me?"

"Yes, ma'am," I reply.

"I don't know, RiAnne," Dallas argues. "I hate to leave you all alone with the new baby. What do you think I should do?"

"I think you should get your ass to London. And as far as staying to celebrate Riley's birthday—" I can hear her whispering but can't hear what she said. She's probably telling him what he's going to owe her. What he owes her, could vary from something sexual to a new car. You never know with those two. When I tease him about it sometimes, he says that she has the toughest, most important, and selfless job in the world—being a mother to their *little hoodlums*. And he truly believes it. A lot of men feel like they are in charge if they are the breadwinners in the family, but not Dallas. He openly worships RiAnne, and says it's why they have a very healthy sex life.

I'm trying to imagine having a wife and kids myself when Dallas says, "I'll pack quick and meet you at the airport."

THE ROYAL SUITE-GEORGETOWN
Knox

IT'S NEARLY TEN by the time we are sated, packed, and fed again. Missy, who will make the trip with us to see to all the details, meets us downstairs.

"Ohmigawd, Missy!" Katie says, wrapping her in a hug before we get in the limo. "You were hilarious! I love you!"

Missy raises an eyebrow at me but succumbs to the hug. Missy tends to be a little hands off when it comes to strangers and personal space. But then Katie says, "So who is your favorite couple?" as we're getting in the car, and the love fest between the two of them begins.

"I'll always love season one, and they are still together, but I will admit I enjoy the drama of some of the newer seasons. Sometimes it seems a little staged, but it's reality TV at its finest, and I admit to being an addict." While they are babbling on about couples, I lean back and close my eyes. I'm fucking exhausted.

I grin to myself. More like exhausted from fucking.

JUAN'S PENTHOUSE TERRACE - SUNSET BOULEVARD
Shelby

"YOU ARE SUCH a goddess." Bam feeds me a grape then proceeds to suck on one of my toes. We're in the bedroom of his hotel penthouse enjoying breakfast after an all-night fuckfest.

We both hear my phone vibrate on the table, but I don't really give a shit who is calling. I'm back in Juan Fabio Martinez's bed, and I couldn't be happier. It's not even the amazing sex. Or the way he says my name. It's the grace and confidence he has as a lover that turns me on.

"I believe your phone is ringing," he says, moving on to the next toe. He glances at the clock, seeing it's nearly five in the morning. "It is an odd time for a conversation. You should make sure it is not of importance."

I take a cursory glance at it and see Riley texted. I pick up the phone and read the message.

> **Riley:** Hey, just wanted to let you know I need to cancel our plans for dinner tonight. I'm heading out of town last minute. I'll call you later and let you know when I'll be back.

I toss the phone down, feeling content. One less thing to worry about.

KEATYN & AIDEN'S HOME–CHELSEA

Knox

"LET THE BACHELOR party begin!" Dallas says when Keatyn and Aiden answer the front door of their new abode.

"As long as Katie comes with us," I say, hugging her.

"What?" Riley says. "No girls allowed at bachelor parties."

"Not even strippers?" Keatyn deadpans, knowing us all too well.

"No way I'm letting this gorgeous thing out of my sight," I tell them.

"We really can't go out," Keatyn says. "Can you imagine the chaos it would create if the press heard Knox and I were seen together when I'm supposed to be on my honeymoon?"

"Even if Aiden and I are there with you?" Katie asks.

"It wouldn't matter," Keatyn replies. "They would crop the two of you out of the picture. They've done it to Aiden for years. It's something you'll just have to get used to. But, the good news is, Marvel arrived a few days ago, and the house is fully stocked with food and drink."

"And just so you know," Aiden continues. "We will definitely be toasting to the end of Knox's bachelor life."

Keatyn gives Katie a hug. "I'm dying to see this ring in person!" Keatyn swoons over the ring, which causes Katie to beam at me. "And we're dying to see this engagement video!"

"We'll get to that," I tell her as she wraps her arms around me. She whispers in my ear, "You did good." Which makes me beam, because I know she's right.

"Where's Missy?" Keatyn asks.

"I booked her, well, she booked herself at the Ritz. And since I made her come here earlier than scheduled, while we go on our honeymoon, her partner Alyssa is flying over to vacation with her."

"Come on in," Aiden says, after we all exchange hugs. "We'll show you around."

"This is gorgeous," Katie gushes.

"This is the formal reception area," Aiden says. "I love it because you can have business meetings here and not encroach on the rest of the home."

"And I'm in love with the lighted art installation in the atrium," Keatyn says. "They are actually supposed to look like falling leaves, but I see feathers. It's like this house was made just for us. Did you notice the name of the house when you were outside?"

"Uh, no," Dallas says.

149

"It's Asher House," Aiden proudly proclaims. "It was the name of the property for centuries before."

"That is really cool," Riley agrees.

"Let's go downstairs," Keatyn says, leading us to the atrium. "Marvel has dinner prepared for us, and then Katie and I will go to the spa for some girl time while you boys," she waves her hand, "do whatever you do. Drink, I guess. Then we can all meet up for dessert."

"But I don't understand," Katie says, "I thought you didn't want to be seen. And what kind of spa is open this time of night?"

"The one here," Keatyn says with a grin.

After we descend the staircase, Aiden shows us the wine gallery, a kitchen, dining and family area. Marvel has snacks set out on the kitchen island, and I suddenly realize I'm starving again.

Aiden opens a couple bottles of bubbly, and we move the party out to the terrace. It's a little cold out, but the fireplace takes the chill off.

"Here's to Knox and Katie," Aiden says, raising his glass. "May you always love each other as recklessly as you do now."

"Here, here," everyone agrees. Katie and I raise our glasses back to them and then take a drink.

Keatyn takes Katie down another level to show her the spa area. I want to go with her, but Dallas grabs the back of my shirt and says, "Oh, no, you don't. The groom needs a shot—or twelve."

"I'm not getting drunk," I state. "I'm getting married to-morrow. But I will have a shot."

A few moments later, those shots turn into two, then three, then four, because the prince decided to join us.

Knox

"WHAT A NIGHT," I say, rolling over.

Katie turns to face me. "How are you feeling?"

"Eh. I'm sorry I got drunk last night. It wasn't my intention. I swear, I usually don't let things get that out of hand."

"I saw the photos in the tabloids of your naked party parade in Vegas and your subsequent mug shot. When was that, again?"

Fuck. "I'm sorry," I say, knowing I sound pathetic. She's not going to want to marry me after this. I don't even want to marry me right now, and I have a pretty high opinion of myself.

"But how can you not when the prince shows up." She's not smiling. I'm fucked. "And when he told us that we couldn't get married at the Register office today, I wanted to drown my sorrows in alcohol too."

"He told us we can't get married? But why not?"

"The place you wanted to get married doesn't do them onsite anymore. Well, you can but it's in a little interview room and only four people total fit. Not exactly Knox-style."

"I don't remember him telling us that," I say, trying to search my brain. I can't believe with all the planning Missy and

I did that we can't get married today. I notice that Katie's not wearing her engagement ring either. That can't be a good sign.

"Do you remember crying?" she asks.

"Why was I crying?"

"Well, blubbering is probably more accurate."

I cover my face with my hands in both frustration and embarrassment. Katie giggles and pries one hand away, surprising me by placing four pain relievers in its place. "Here take these and drink this," she says, handing me a bottle of water. Maybe she doesn't hate me.

"Oh, I love you."

She giggles. "I know that for sure now."

I narrow my eyes at her.

The sound of her laughter is like angels singing in the heavens, even with my massive headache. "Yes, that's what you were blubbering about. How much you love me."

"You look happy about that," I observe.

"Well, I was a little nervous about all of this happening so fast. It's scary trusting someone you've just met."

"And now you're not nervous?"

"I'm not nervous about marrying you. I'm excited about it. I can't wait, Knox."

"Except we can't get married?" I ask, my brain a little foggy this morning.

"We're getting married but—get this—it will be at Kensington Palace!"

"At the Palace?"

"Yeah, don't you remember asking the prince if you could borrow one of his crowns for the wedding?"

"Uh, no."

"You were funny. Keatyn said you were in rare form. I don't know if that's good or bad, but you made me laugh. Especially when you challenged the prince to a duel."

"A duel?" I ask, rubbing my hand across my face, hoping it

will bring back some memory of all this.

"Yeah, with swords, except no one had any of those handy so you used sticks." She runs her hand across my check which I realize is sore from a cut.

"You're lucky you didn't take out your eye. Didn't your mom ever teach you not to run with a stick, especially when you're drunk?"

"That I do remember her telling me. I must not have listened."

She wrinkles up her cute little button nose and grimaces. "How's your ass?"

"Katie! What did you do to my ass when I was drunk?" I'm appalled she'd take advantage of me. And if she did, why am I not lucky enough to remember?

"It wasn't me. It was the prince."

I have a moment of terror imagining the things another man could do to my ass.

"Uh, what did he do, exactly?"

"Oh, Knox," she says, giving me a playful slap on the arm. "You have a dirty mind. You and the prince did not have anal sex, although that might have been kind of hot to watch. You really don't remember falling on your ass? It has to hurt. Maybe you're still numb from all the alcohol."

I reach back and rub a sore butt cheek, instantly remembering falling on it.

"Did I fall?"

"You told everyone you were going to scale the castle wall."

"Oh, Lord. Sounds like a theme."

"Yes, you were pretending to be my knight or something because you thought the prince was flirting with me. That's what caused you to challenge him to a duel."

"Was he flirting with you?"

She grins. "Maybe a little, but I think he flirts with everyone."

"True," I agree. "Aiden and I have been with him on what he calls a *bender*, or drinking spree before. He's a natural born flirt."

"I can tell. So anyway, you tried to scale Keatyn and Aiden's terrace wall. You slipped. Fell from about six feet up straight onto your ass. I tried to stop you. You told me you were a trained professional and do most of your own stunts."

"I'm embarrassed." I roll my head into her chest and sigh. "Listening to your heartbeat makes me not hear mine hammering in my head."

"I smell food," she says. "I don't know what they are cooking, but it smells like greasy cheeseburgers and possibly bacon. It smells divine, and you probably need to eat. I'm surprised you haven't gotten sick with all you drank."

I don't lift my head up. I can't face her. "Did you have fun last night?" Please say yes. Please say I didn't ruin everything. "Do you still want to marry me?"

"Yes, I had fun. Keatyn and I had girl time. It's been forever since we just relaxed and talked like that. I really miss her and Maggie. We've stayed close through texts and visits when we can, but I would like to live closer to them. Keatyn even mentioned I should consider writing scripts instead of books or both, that she wouldn't be opposed to doing a few movies more geared toward children."

"You didn't answer the other part," I say nervously.

She runs her fingers through my hair. "Knox Daniels, I knew you had a wild side. I like it and I love you. Of course, I still want to marry you."

"Whew. I was so afraid I screwed everything up." My nose perks up, smelling food, too. "You know, that food does smell good."

"Then let's get up and get our wedding day started."

WE GET UP, use the bathroom, and brush our teeth. I notice

two robes hanging on a hook. "Here, let's just wear these."

"Okay," she says, tossing one over her delicious nakedness. I notice a large hickey just on the side of her boob.

I pull her against me. "Did you take advantage of me last night?"

"I most certainly did." She grins. "Do you not remember that either?"

"I remember you smelled really good. I remember wanting you."

"It's really too bad you don't remember. I was worried— sometimes when a guy is drunk things don't work quite right."

"It worked though," I say brightening, flashes of doing her on the bathroom counter flooding my memory. "We did it right here. I remember watching your tits bounce in the mirror."

"Oh, yes. That was just one of the places we did it. You were pretty impressive. It was like you'd taken a Viagra or something. Did you?"

"No!"

"You said it was whiskey dick. I always thought that meant a guy couldn't get it up."

"We were drinking Irish whiskey. Makes a man stand at attention all night long," I tease.

"Well, it worked. Quite well. And we're taking a whole bunch of whatever it was that you drank with us on the honeymoon."

"YOU'RE UP AND alive!" Keatyn says loudly when we arrive in the kitchen. "Feeling foxy, Knoxy?"

"Shut up," I say, holding my head.

"I told you to shut up a few times, last night, Knox. But you didn't listen," she says. "I also tried to save you from yourself. Although you aren't the only one who isn't feeling great this morning. Aiden and Riley were both throwing up last night."

"Well, at least I didn't puke. Guess I can handle my liquor

better than them," I say, sitting up straighter.

"The perfect hangover food." She shoves a plate in front of each of us. "Greasy bacon cheeseburger, Marvel's homemade *frites*, and a bloody Mary."

"That looks amazing," I say, digging in.

Katie sits down next to me and does the same. "Is everyone else still asleep?" she asks.

"Not me," Dallas says from behind us. I just now notice he's sitting at the dining table next to the kitchen reading the paper. "You should know that I took numerous videos of you last night. Had to share them with the missus."

"You took videos of me drunk to show RiAnne?"

"Yep," he smirks. "She's quite proud of me. Thanks for being so entertaining. I just earned major bonus points with my wife."

"How is my getting drunk earning you points?"

"Do you remember my wedding?"

"Yes, I was so fucking hungover. Hell, I may have still been drunk," I say.

"Payback is a bitch," Dallas says calmly. "Or so my wife believes."

"That was like ten years ago," Katie giggles. Keatyn busts out laughing, too.

"There's a good life lesson for you, Knox," Dallas says. "Women are like elephants. They don't forget a thing. And they *never* forget when you fuck up. So my marriage advice to you is don't fuck up."

I can't help but laugh along with them.

"So, while you boys recover, I'm taking Katie downstairs. Missy arranged for hair and makeup." She glances at her watch. "It's one o'clock now. We'll be ready to leave for the palace at four. That means you will be dressed and ready by then, too." She gives Dallas a glare. "And paybacks are officially over, correct?"

"Yes, ma'am," he says. "Today is all about the celebration."

"I can't believe you're getting married at Kensington Palace. That is so incredibly cool."

"Have you ever been there?" Katie asks Keatyn.

"Actually, yes. We were at a wedding held at the Orangery there a couple years ago. And we've been to a fundraiser the prince held there. The grounds are beautiful. Your photos will be amazing. Although, I believe you're going to be married in one of the private gardens on the property. The Orangery is open for breakfast, lunch, and afternoon tea, and the prince certainly understands your need for privacy."

"I feel like I'm living a fairytale," Katie says, causing me to almost blush. She finishes eating then gives me a kiss on the cheek and says, "The next time I see you, I'll be walking down the aisle."

"Wow," I say, the full force of what I'm about to do weighing on me.

After she and Keatyn leave the room, Dallas says, "You sure this is the right thing, Knox? What about a pre-nup? Do you need me to draw one up?"

"I didn't even think about that."

"It's my job as your friend, to remind you of that." He stands. "Let's go get some fresh air. You could probably use some."

"Yeah, I could," I reply, following him out to the terrace. When I sit down, I realize my ass does really hurt. I can't help but rub it.

"You took a pretty good fall," Dallas says with a laugh. "I'll have to show you the highlight reel. I'm surprised you're moving around as good as you are today."

"I think I'm still numb," I tease. "Dallas, do you think this is a bad idea? I'm really surprised no one has tried to talk me out of it."

"It helps that we all know Katie and know what kind of

person she is. We know she's not marrying you for your money. She's had a lot of men want to marry her before, but she always said they were never the one, and she didn't want to settle. I don't believe she would be going through with this if she wasn't confident that you were it."

"I'm crazy in love with her. We're extremely compatible in the bedroom, but it's so much more than that. I feel like I'm starring in one of those gushy love stories Keatyn writes. I just can't wait to spend the rest of my life with her. Do you think I need a pre-nup?"

"I think everyone with significant assets going into a marriage needs one, but I didn't come up with the idea. She asked me about it last night."

"Asked if I would ask her to sign one?"

"No, she asked me to draft one. She said you hadn't said anything, and she didn't feel right about it. She doesn't want your money, Knox. She wants your love, and she has your best interests at heart."

"God, that makes me love her even more. So what should I do?"

"That's up to you."

"Do Keatyn and Aiden have one?"

"They have a financial agreement that covers how any monies split upon a divorce or even death will be handled. Their biggest worry, honestly, is that if they have children and the other gets remarried, is to protect their children's assets."

"That makes sense. I'd like something like that."

"Are you thinking about children?"

"Actually, yes. We both want them. Probably not right away. I want to enjoy having her to myself for a couple years. Travel, show her the world."

"Why don't I talk to Katie about it, since you aren't supposed to see her until the ceremony. If she agrees, we'll handle everything as part of your estate planning. You know, if you were marrying anyone other than Katie, I would be handling this very differently."

"That makes me happy," I tell him.

"Why?"

"Because I trust you, Dallas. And you believe in her as much as I do."

I contemplate calling my mother and telling her what I'm about to do, but I think I'd rather ask forgiveness later than answer the million questions she's sure to ask.

"How's it hanging?" Riley says, stepping out onto the terrace with a cheeseburger in one hand and a plate stacked with more food in the other.

"Dallas, did you even get drunk?" I ask.

"No, I did not. I was too busy live streaming your shenanigans to my lovely bride."

Riley breaks out in laughter, but then sets the food on the table and holds his head. "Laughing hurts my brain. Whose idea was it to invite the prince?"

"Mine," Aiden says, joining us with a similar plate full of food. He's also carrying a bottle of whiskey under his arm.

"Oh, no. No more of that!" I say, holding my hands in the air in defeat. "Trust me, the whiskey won last night. I don't need a second round."

"Hair of the dog," Aiden says, ignoring my protests and pouring shots in the glasses Marvel just brought out on a tray.

"How can you even stand to smell that shit?" Riley asks.

"It sure tastes better going down than it does coming up," Aiden agrees. "But this is the only way to cure a whiskey hangover. Or so the prince tells me."

"He's full of shit," Riley argues, but he still takes one of the glasses and raises it into the air. "Here's to those who wish us well. Those who don't can go to hell."

We all drink and then Aiden mutters, "We may already be in hell."

"Aiden, I'm shocked. You don't usually drink that much."

"I know. I don't know what got into me."

"Irish whiskey," the rest of us say with a laugh.

Marvel brings out platters of more food for us, but before we eat, Aiden pours us each another shot. "I think we all need to toast the groom."

"Aren't we supposed to do that after the wedding?"

"Wait!" Missy says, running out onto the terrace. "I'm playing photographer today. We'll want to capture this moment."

"I'm in a bathrobe," I mutter.

"I don't care how hungover you are, Knox Daniels, you will smile for the camera. You want to have photos to remember your wedding day."

I stop slouching and nod to her.

"Okay, Aiden, go ahead," she says, camera at the ready.

We raise our glasses in the air again, and Aiden says, "Knox, may all your ups and downs be between the sheets."

Dallas roars with laughter.

MISSY RUNS BACK and forth between the guys and the girls taking photos. We've moved from the terrace to the salon and are playing pool when she announces that it's time for us to go get ready. We'll be leaving for the palace in a half hour. When I step out of the shower and into my room, she's steaming the wrinkles out of my tuxedo.

"How does she look?" I ask her.

"Katie looks stunning. The more I get to know her, the more I like her. You made a good choice, Knox. Have you called your mother?"

"No. I thought about it, but I figured maybe it would be better to call her on our honeymoon."

"Well, the last thing you want is for her to find out in the papers and not from you."

"Yeah, I suppose you are right. Any chance we can keep it out of the papers?"

"I think so. At least until we are ready to announce it. The makeup and hair people who are prepping her and Keatyn believe it's for an event of Keatyn's. They don't even know that you are here. The prince assured me that things will be kept hush on their end. But I still think you owe your mother a call."

"Yeah, you're right." She hands me my phone, my mother's cell number already dialed.

"Knox, sweetie, how are you?" my mother asks. I immediately get choked up.

"Hey, Mom. How's Haiti treating you?"

"Oh, Knox, we're doing such good work here. But I'll be ready to see you over the holidays. I miss you."

"I miss you, too. Uh, mom, I have something I need to tell you."

"What's wrong? Are you okay?"

"Yes, I'm fine."

"Is Keatyn okay?"

"Yes, everyone is okay. I wanted to tell you that I met someone."

"I assume you meet people every day, Knox. Are you referring to a girl? Someone special?"

"Yes, her name is Katie. She's a friend of Keatyn's. We actually met at their wedding. And I've been seeing her since."

"I saw the news about their wedding on the internet. That was last week, right?"

"Yeah, um, Mom. Katie and I are eloping today. I'm getting married."

"Knox Nathan Daniels. What are you thinking?"

"I'm thinking I'm crazy, madly in love with this girl, and I want to make it official. I just wanted you to hear it from me. And I'm super excited for you to meet her."

"Sorry, I'm a little shocked by all this. Are you sure it's the right thing? You're not drunk are you?"

"No, Mom. If anything I'm drunk on love."

"Well, that's sort of romantic. Will you at least send me a picture?"

"I will, but promise me you won't show anyone for a week. Until we announce it to the press."

"Agreed. Well, I guess congratulations are in order."

"Thanks, Mom. I love you."

"I love you, too, son. Does this mean I might have grand-children some day?"

"Absolutely."

"Well, then I'm warming to this idea already."

"Phew," I say, hanging up.

"Sounds like she took it well?" Missy asks.

"Yeah, I think so. She was shocked, but I know she'll love Katie when she meets her. And she's been wanting grandkids for quite a while now. All her friends are grandmothers already. I told her just a few weeks ago not to hold her breath. Amazing how quickly your life can change."

"I'll say," she agrees. "Just a few days ago, I never imagined I'd be spending the week in London with my love."

"You two have fun. And thank you for everything you've done this week. What do you think of Katie's dress?"

"I think you have a gorgeous bride. And it has nothing to do with what she's wearing, Knox."

"Thank you," I say, feeling grateful.

"And please, I heard all about last night. No more shots for you, no matter what your friends say."

"You gonna whoop on them if they try?"

"Hell, yeah. They don't wanna mess with Missy."

"I hear that," I tease.

She smacks my butt. "I'm leaving. Get your ass in your tux and get out to the car."

I give her a salute as she walks out the door.

NEXT THING I know, I'm standing at the far end of a beautiful garden. The brick walls are covered in vines and moss giving it a storybook feel. Tucked into the vines are richly hued English cabbage roses, peonies, and sweet peas in deep rich reds, purples, and pinks. There is an arch at the end creating an altar covered with more of the flowers. Red rose petals are sprinkled on the ground to form a path to the altar. A lone violinist is playing a romantic tune.

Aiden cups my shoulder with his hand. "You ready?"

"Yeah. I just realized. Missy forgot to give me the wedding rings."

"I have them in my pocket. You really think Missy would forget that?"

"Yeah, you're right. She wouldn't. Were you nervous at your wedding, Aiden?"

He shakes his head. "I'd say I felt a lot of nervous excitement. I couldn't wait to watch her walk down the aisle and I couldn't wait for her to be my wife."

"Why did you wait so long?"

"Because she said being married didn't matter to her. That all that mattered was that we were together. But I wanted more. And I suspected she did, too."

"I figured as much. Are you glad you did it?"

"I'm very glad. You getting cold feet?" he asks.

"A little."

"They will go away the second you see her at the end of the aisle. If they don't, you run, I'll take the flack."

The thought of running away from Katie turns my stomach. It's not that I don't want to marry her, it's more like I have a case of stage fright, which is something I've never experienced.

But Aiden's right. The second I see her, it's gone. She looks beautiful. Gorgeous. Stunning. I try to pay attention to her dress, because I know the dress is a big deal to women, but I barely notice that it's anything more than white. It's the total picture of her. White dress, short veil, beaming smile, bouquet of red roses. The way her eyes lock on mine. The way they bring tears to them. I don't think I've ever been happier than this. This gorgeous creature is going to be my wife, and that makes me incredibly blessed.

Our ceremony is short and sweet. We hold hands, repeat our vows, and are pronounced husband and wife. I don't even wait for the officiant to say it. I dip Katie back and give her a dramatic first, married couple kiss.

After the ceremony, a waiter brings champagne on a silver platter, and I make a toast to my beautiful bride.

"Katie, I want to share a quote with you that my dad shared with me when I got my first acting role. Eleanor Roosevelt once said that 'The future belongs to those who believe in the beauty of their dreams.' At the time, I thought it related to achieving my dream of becoming an actor, but now I understand it so much better. *You* are my future, Katie, because you are the beauty of my dreams."

Katie's eyes fill with tears as I clink her flute and drink in her honor.

"Knox," she says, "You swept me off my feet from the start. From our first kiss, to my first helicopter ride, to the most outrageous proposal anyone has ever dreamed up, to asking me to elope, to getting married at a palace made me believe in something I didn't think I'd ever find—true love." She throws her glass up in the air. "Everyone toast to my new sexy-as-hell husband!"

I look out at my friends, Keatyn, Aiden, Riley, Dallas, Missy, and even the damn prince. And know I'm finally getting everything my father ever dreamed of for me.

TUESDAY, OCTOBER 28TH
BAM'S YACHT – PACIFIC OCEAN

Shelby

I'M SITTING ON a yacht—a freaking, huge-ass, floating hotel of a yacht. The thing is incredible. Juan gave me a brief tour when we arrived, acting like all this excess is normal.

I guess for him, it probably is.

"So what do you think of my boat?" he asks.

"I've never seen such extravagance and wealth all on display in one place," I answer honestly.

"You should see our family castles."

"You have castles, as in plural?"

"Yes, we have one in Argentina, where our family mining business started. And one—"

"What do you mine?" I interrupt.

"Everything. Copper, gold, silver, zinc. Things like natural gas, crude petroleum, uranium, cadmium, and lithium."

"Are you telling me you *own* a gold mine?"

"Yes, of course," he says with a sexy laugh, like it's the most common thing in the world. Like saying you own a coffee maker. "Would you desire a glass of champagne?"

"Is it good champagne?" I joke.

"Everything I surround myself with is of the finest money can buy, of that you can be assured."

"Then, yes, I would love some." He snaps a finger, and a waiter dressed in all white immediately returns with a bottle of champagne in what looks to be a real silver champagne bucket—probably silver from his freaking mine.

"You are a funny girl, no? You are teasing me about my wealth. That is—uncommon."

I can't help but laugh. "Let's just say my family was not wealthy."

"But, yet, you do not seem like—what is the saying—a gold digger."

"I used to proudly consider myself a gold digger. That was my goal. I thought if I married a man with money, all my problems would disappear. Then I met a man with money. He wasn't into monogamy and I was okay with that because I don't think one man could ever keep me sexually satisfied. But, I told myself I was in love with him because of the things he could give me. Things I'd never be able to possess on my own, probably. And he took care of me. Put me up at the hotel where we met." I let out a sigh. I don't know why I'm telling him all this. He will probably kick me off his boat. It's clear he's just looking for a good time. Like Riley. "But then I realized I want more than money. I want more than just sex. I want a man to shower me with his attention, with his love. Would I like gifts? Sure, but I want them to mean something, you know? Like I'd rather have a diamond chip from a man who worked to save for it, just for me, than a carat from someone who bought it with no thought."

Juan smiles at me, hands me a flute, and raises his into the air. "To the most romantic soul I have ever had the pleasure of meeting. Salud."

He takes a drink, but I don't. "What does *salud* mean?"

"It means *to your health* in Spanish, similar to *cheers*."

"Oh, that's nice. Salud," I say, thinking about my baby and wondering if I should be drinking this. I take a polite sip then set the glass down.

"I want to learn more about you. Tell me."

"There is not much to tell. I had a crappy childhood. Moved out with some guy as soon as I could and have been on my own ever since. I was working as a cocktail waitress, and like everyone else who comes to Hollywood, I was waiting for my big break."

"You want to be an actress?"

"I thought so. Now, I don't know what I want."

"Your relationship with the man with money, is it over?"

"It can't be because I quit my job for him and have nowhere to go. So basically, I'm fucked."

"Join the club," Juan says, downing his champagne and pouring himself another. "My father is gravely ill. I am the eldest son, and it is my duty to take over our business holdings and provide for my family when he passes. Which will be soon. That means I must retire from polo, a game I have spent my lifetime perfecting—the game I love."

"You're quitting polo?" I ask, a little devastated. I was hoping to go to a match with him.

"Yes. I must stop my playboy ways, marry in the church, and produce an heir. Considering my last girlfriend dumped me for a younger man and my ex-wife did not succumb to my charms a second time, I am going to fail my family. It may sound silly to an American, but in my culture, family is everything. And I have been given a great responsibility."

"I'm pregnant," I blurt out. Shit. Why did I just say that?

He squints his eyes, thinking. "And the rich man is the baby's father?"

"This makes me sound horrible, but I met this man just after I learned I was pregnant. I was devastated. This guy was all VIP and I needed an escape from daily life. I only planned on it being a one-night stand. But he swept me off my feet, took me on his private jet to parties around the world. I got caught up in it and in him. Then some girl who broke his heart like ten years ago, who was still married, came back into his life and wanted to get back together with him. In my mind, I was protecting him from her. By that time, I had missed work, got fired, and got kicked out of my apartment. I was desperate, so I told him it was his. The baby's real father was a bartender. He doesn't even know I'm pregnant and wouldn't want to have anything do with the baby."

"What's his heritage?"

"The baby's father?"

"Yes."

"Um, his father was from Ecuador and his mother was from Argentina."

"Interesting. How far along are you?"

"Eleven weeks," I admit. "That's the other thing. I don't think the guy with money will be thrilled to learn I am pregnant with someone else's child. He's kind of an ass."

"I'm kind of an ass, too," Juan says, laughing. "Or so I am told. But I'm going to change that. It is important to me."

"You're one of the nicest human beings I have ever met," I tell him, sincerely.

"Then clearly, I have you fooled," he teases. "I like that about you."

I smile. He's flirting with and teasing me. It's like everything he does, every breath of air he takes, is part of one long stretch of foreplay.

He asks the waiter guy to bring me some sparkling water and a lime. Then he says, "Will you please excuse me?" He points to the chaises on the sun deck. "Why don't you relax? I will be back momentarily."

I wait for a whole lot of moments and start wondering if he's jumped ship.

Guess that's what I get for being honest.

The End

About the Author

Jillian is a *USA TODAY* bestselling author who writes fun romances with characters her readers fall in love with, from the boy next door in the *That Boy* trilogy to the daughter of a famous actress in *The Keatyn Chronicles* to a kick-ass young assassin in the *Spy Girl* series.

She lives in a small Florida beach town, is married to her college sweetheart, has two grown children, and two Labrador Retrievers named Cali and Camber. When she's not working, she likes to travel, paint, shop for shoes, watch football, and go to the beach.

Check out Jillian's website at www.jilliandodd.net for added content and to sign up for her newsletter.

Made in the USA
Columbia, SC
20 March 2021